MANAGED CARE

MANAGED CARE

A Novel

By

David Milofsky

BryanDorsey Books
Denver

ISBN: 154482291X
ISBN 13: 9781544822914

Also by David Milofsky

A Friend of Kissinger

Color of Law

Eternal People

Playing From Memory

To Jeanie, of course.

ACKNOWLEDGMENTS

I wish to acknowledge my debt to the National Endowment for the Arts and to the MacDowell Colony for fellowships granted during the writing of this book. I am also grateful to the editors of TriQuarterly, Prairie Schooner, Beloit Fiction Journal and The Bellevue Literary Review for publishing sections of this novel in somewhat different form.

In addition I am grateful to the following physicians who, often without knowing it, allowed me into their professional lives and in the process enlarged my knowledge of the art of medicine: Mark Linkow, Amy Solar Mills, Kim Schurman, David Hurst, John Kelly, Roy Lowenstein, Ruth Nauts, Joe Craft, Barbara Dutmers, Rick Cohn, Ed Gibson, Gary May, David Hahn, Marc Sorkin, Henry Coppalillo, Hubert Thomason, Steve Bishop, Dewey Walker, Barton Schmitt, Rick Abrams, Frank Guerra, David Bender, Ellis Ellison, Evan Ellison, Jim Ellison, David Ellison, David Thaler, Joe Thaler, Bill Finch, James Crow, Marty Blazer, Jules Amer, Deborah Shaw, Liz Kincannon, Jandell Allen-Davis, Danielle Ofri, Patty Fahey, Kareem Sobky, Jennifer Hoffman, Jonathan Hoffman and the late Allan Milofsky.

For personal encouragement I want to thank my friends Ronna Wineberg, M.K. Malik, Barbara Wright, Frank Gay and the late George Cuomo. Finally, Joyce Meskis and Cathy Langer of the Tattered Cover Bookstore have helped me in countless ways and, more important, helped build and establish a literary community in Denver. I am grateful.

"The poet is the true and only doctor"—Emerson

"First, do no harm,"—Hippocratic oath

CHAPTER ONE

June in Colorado and uncharacteristically chilly. Thunderheads bordered by orange shots of lightning hung on the horizon like sullen bullies waiting to let loose with rain, hail, tornados or all three at once. Just like my life, Sylvia Rose thought. It was the uneasy balance between calm and sudden violence that resonated. Still, Denver had its advantages. Unlike California, where she had grown up, there was no humidity and she liked the smell of summer rain even if she couldn't really smell anything cocooned as she was behind the Thermopane windows of her office on the seventeenth floor of the medical building.

The intercom buzzed on the desk behind her. "Your patient's here, doctor," the secretary said. "I'll be a few minutes," Sylvia replied.

She took a deep breath. This was the moment she treasured, before the onslaught of the day, the brief time she had to herself before she would have to face ten or fifteen patients, few of whom she'd be able to encourage or even treat. It was the fate of neurologists everywhere. Her cases were supposed to represent intellectual challenges and they did. But for Sylvia it had never been that simple. Still, she found her anxiety and sweaty palms embarrassing since she was the one in whom calm certainty was supposed to reside.

Now she glanced at the neatly typed schedule of patients on her desk and shook her head to clear her mind of memories. She had to focus. She was surprised to see Thomas Morris' name was first on the list. Normally, Sylvia wasn't impressed by celebrity because ill patients tended to take on their own identities quickly and leave behind whatever they had been in the world.

This was different, though, at least to Sylvia. She had listened to his work on the local NPR station and seen him perform twice. When they met, however, she was struck that he seemed smaller in person than he had at the concert in black tie and tails.

I've heard you play," she said after shaking hands. "Last year, at the University." And then she was at a loss. Neither of them had expected him to be in her office, less than a year after that concert.

Thomas seemed accustomed to being recognized and sought to put his doctor at ease before she had even examined him. "I've had a blessed life," he said. It was an unusual opener, but as he talked, Sylvia had to admit, he was right. Born with natural gifts, he was fortunate to have prosperous parents who afforded him the best training from an early age. After graduation from Curtis and his debut at Town Hall, he had begun touring, which is how he met his wife. Yet now, at thirty-two, he found himself unable to stay upright for any period of time without experiencing vertigo. Physical activity exhausted him and he said his joints felt as if they were welded together and the welds weren't holding.

Most patients weren't so creative, Sylvia thought. It was hard enough getting them to describe their symptoms accurately without adding artistic flourishes. But when she examined Thomas, she discovered he had a low-grade fever and swollen glands in his neck. "Anything else?" she asked, brisk in the extreme without knowing why.

Morris didn't seem to react. He smiled brilliantly at her. "Yes," he said. "While I was shaving, I noticed this bright red rash around my cheekbones, just below my eyes. When I smeared on cold cream, the rash only became worse."

"He looked like a fox," his wife said. "First, we went to his primary care doctor who sent us to a dermatologist but Tommy didn't have the rash that day. Then because he was dizzy and losing his balance all the time, they said we should see a neurologist." She shrugged and looked at Sylvia. "That's why we came to you."

A tall, plain woman in a black sheath, she had been quiet until now, but mention of the rash seemed to energize her. Mrs. Morris spoke in the matter-of-fact way she might have announced their arrival at soccer practice, but Sylvia was used to this. For most patients illness was an unwelcome guest. Mrs Morris was doing her best to ward it off by maintaining an aloof disinterest, as if what was going on was happening to someone other than her husband.

"It wasn't a very good concert," Thomas said now, apparently unconcerned by his wife's listing of his symptoms. But Sylvia knew he was right. He had been playing with the local symphony whose conductor had a suspicion of anything written after 1900. "Do you play yourself?" Morris asked suddenly. "An instrument?"

Sylvia flushed, embarrassed that he had seemed to intuit her unusual interest but pleased he had asked. "Not any more,' she said. "I studied the piano when I was growing up, before I decided to go to medical school." The truth was that Sylvia had always dreamed of being a musician. Even now she flattered herself to the extent that she believed she might have been a professional but for a combination of inadequate instruction and unseeing parents who had pointed her in other directions.

As Thomas looked at her intently, it seemed as if he were looking at a spot just over Sylvia's right shoulder. She noticed a slight tremor in his cheek. "What's happening to me?" he asked plaintively. "I look like a teen-ager with this face, but I feel like I'm going to fall on my face when I try to walk any distance."

"I don't know yet," Sylvia had said. "But we're going to find out."

Now, looking west toward Broadway far below, she saw the strange yellow articulated wall a sculptor had erected there, a huge concrete exclamation point interrupting the mountain view. Like much of Denver, the original had been created somewhere else then replicated downtown, a transplant, as Sylvia was, as were most of the people she knew here. No one seemed to be from Colorado; everyone gravitated here because of the mountains, summer skiing, the endless sunshine, god knew why.

The world she looked down on was peaceful and orderly, cars moving sedately along the street, the tiny pedestrians busy on their way. It was altogether a beautiful morning, much too nice to be thinking about divorce, yet this was on Sylvia's mind, as it had been obsessively for months, even years, almost since her honeymoon when she looked across the bed at Mitchell in a dim Venice hotel room and wondered why she'd gotten married. She hadn't said anything to him, of course. What was there to say? "Sorry, but I've just decided I don't really love you." They were newlyweds. Get used to it, she told herself and so she had.

After Thomas left, Sylvia stood looking out the window at the dark and lowering clouds on the horizon for ten minutes without registering what she was seeing. She was committed to her patients but there were also her husband and children to consider. Between carpools and putting a meal on the table each evening, she knew she'd be a better mother if she didn't think as much about life-threatening diseases. Yet the distance that eluded her where it should serve, in her medical practice, was all too easily achieved at home, with her husband. She felt as distant from Mitchell and their life together as from the case files that cascaded off her desk and onto the floor.

In the beginning, she had hoped her feelings of regret about the marriage would lessen, that she'd adjust and even come to love and value her husband. Rather than fading, however, the malaise continued and gradually increased in intensity, leaving her where she was now: paralyzed by anxiety and miserable because of it. And yet there was nothing overtly wrong with her husband; other women actually found him attractive. His light brown hair was going gray but he was slim, dressed well, and was gifted in social situations for finding the thing that every other guest valued most about themselves and asking questions about it. Although Mitchell had cultivated an attenuated style that made some suspect there was something mysterious about him, in fact, Mitchell was the most uncomplicated person Sylvia knew. It was just that he understood that getting people to talk about themselves was the most essential aspect of social life. This had served him well and resulted in constant invitations to parties, benefits, concerts and the like. It also benefited him in his job as a representative for an east coast suit manufacturer, a position that required almost constant travel and thus distance from his wife and family.

She had a patient waiting, but something about the meeting with Thomas Morris had disturbed her. She didn't think it was just the pathos of his situation, nor the seriousness of his diagnosis, for she had many patients who were sicker than Thomas. She was aware of where he was headed and how much worse he would get, but that was always the case. She knew when to withhold information from a patient that would not help and might cause him additional distress.

She didn't think Thomas's place in the musical world inhibited her, for she had treated celebrities before. Once a famous television newsman had appeared with his wife in her examining room and another time she had conducted grand rounds at a neurological hospital where they were treating a jockey with a broken back who had once won the Kentucky Derby. Illness had a democratizing effect on everyone.

It had been drummed into Sylvia in medical school to think of her patients as cases, not people with families and careers. This made sense. How could she do her job, provide the best diagnosis and treatment if she was constantly caught up in the drama of their lives? The difficulty was in combining this with the compassion that was so important in treating patients. Usually Sylvia was able to make this work reflexively, to keep herself paradoxically involved yet uninvolved, but now she worried that she might be losing her grip.

The phone interrupted her thoughts and Sylvia picked up to discover with some annoyance that it was her husband. Mitchell had a habit of clearing his throat as if he were going to make an important pronouncement then following this with some triviality. He cleared his throat and said, "How are you?"

Disappointed as usual, Sylvia thought, but she said, "A patient I hadn't seen for a while told me I look older."

She didn't know why she was telling Mitchell this; she hadn't thought it bothered her at the time. It just came out. But Mitchell sighed and said gloomily, "Well, it's true. We're all getting older."

Sylvia fought her irritation. She wanted Mitchell to protest, to tell her she was youthful and beautiful and hadn't changed since the day they met. Whatever the truth might be, she wanted him to see her in an ideal light. Someone had to start to change things between them. Perhaps he could suggest dinner and a movie. Instead he merely agreed and now she *felt* old.

Yet even as all this ran through her mind, Sylvia knew her expectations were unreasonable. She should accept her husband as he was. Who really changed his personality after thirty? A friend had once unkindly suggested that she should be happy because

Mitchell was the perfect wife and would never interfere by making unreasonable demands on her time. Sylvia knew professional women who often complained aloud that this was exactly what they needed. She didn't know if she needed a wife or not; she only knew she didn't want one. "Did you need something?" she asked a little sharply.

Mitchell cleared his throat again and Sylvia could see his close-set eyes and rabbit-teeth, the wrinkles in his forehead, the dome of his head through the few strands of hair he painstakingly arranged each morning at the mirror. "It's just that I have a meeting this afternoon," Mitchell said carefully. "I was wondering if you could pick up Becky at day care?"

Sylvia knew Mitchell's meetings usually consisted of his sitting with friends at the Jewish Community Center drinking tea and discussing the latest conflicts in Israel or the Jewish community. Mitchell was the scion of one of the most important Jewish families in Denver and most of his friends had similar biographies. His grandparents had started a mid-level clothing store that quickly grew into a small chain with franchises in several other western cities. Mitchell had gone east to college and nurtured ideas of being an academic before leaving after receiving his masters in philosophy. When Sylvia quizzed him on this, he had said, "I just realized that I could go away for twenty years and Plato would still be there."

This would have been the attraction to some young scholars, but for Mitchell it led to a deep depression that resulted in his returning to Denver. He was first a silent partner in the family business with his two brothers, but in time he started working as a traveler, an arrangement that was supposed to be temporary, but had now lasted fifteen years.

Sylvia had little respect for business, but she had found Mitchell attractive when they met, in part because what she understood to be his family's social standing was so different from her own. They represented a kind of Jewish aristocracy and Mitchell's bearing and sense of himself reflected this.

There was never any passion in the relationship; Mitchell wasn't a passionate person as he'd be the first to admit, but in the beginning he talked aimlessly about returned to school to study law or accounting, ideas that fell by the wayside until over time he settled into his current position. It was useless to argue about whose life was more important and Sylvia knew this wasn't really the issue anyway.

"What's wrong with him?" her mother demanded during one visit. "He's a very nice young man, from a good family, you have no financial problems and he plays a wonderful game of tennis. Very graceful."

"He dresses well too," Sylvia added before adding, "I don't know. He just doesn't have any zip."

"Zip?" her mother said, incredulous. "You're thinking about leaving your husband because he doesn't have zip?"

She hadn't actually thought about leaving until her mother mentioned it, but she'd been able to think of little else since. She knew they stayed together for the children and she felt perennially guilty about how little time she spent with them.

She heard Mitchell's breathing on the line and glanced quickly at her calendar. She had an open hour at four, enough time to drive across town, buy her daughter ice-cream and depending on traffic get back to the hospital in time for rounds at five. It was important to avoid feeling overwhelmed, even if life was overwhelming. "I can do that," she said quickly, and hung up.

Sylvia was barely in time to pick up her daughter who stood, transferring her weight from one foot to the other in front of the old brick building. Becky wore an expression that Sylvia recognized and communicated anxiety that neither parent would make it there in time, a small vertical line in her forehead that broke Sylvia's heart. There was nothing worse than being the last child waiting for her mother. Whatever her other failings, it was a point of honor with Sylvia to be on time when it was her turn to drive. The little girl jumped up and down, smiling when she saw her mother in the old Volvo.

"How was school?" Sylvia asked when Becky was in the car.

Becky was small and brown from the sun with little black eyes in a round face. She wrapped her arms tightly around Sylvia's neck. "Normal," she said.

Sylvia considered her daughter's words for a moment. How nice it would be if she were able to be as satisfied as her daughter with normality, if she didn't continue to feel there were unseen heights she should be ascending, further indications of brilliance and achievement. Wouldn't it be wonderful if she were able to take her foot off the accelerator and coast? But normality had never really been a significant part of her life and this was unlikely to change. "Normal good or normal bad?" she asked, probing a bit.

Becky shrugged. "Just normal. Can we get ice cream?

CHAPTER TWO

Sylvia looked at the blue paper on her desk. The words swam in her vision and made no sense. She was being called to an M&M, an investigation hospitals were obliged to conduct into unexpected deaths, a good thing. But what did it have to do with her? She hadn't killed anyone, hadn't made more than the usual number of mistakes. Still, she immediately felt guilty because she knew she was always moving too fast, juggling too much. As a result, in her mind, the occurrence of some grievous disaster was only a matter of time. Why not today?

She re-read the letter. Slowly it came into focus and she remembered. It had been a Tuesday and Sylvia was putting in the half-day at the clinic required of all staff physicians when she was called to see a patient complaining of lower-back pain. Sylvia entered the exam room to find a middle-aged white man with wild, staring eyes, shivering in a light gown. "You're a woman," he said.

Sylvia offered her hand. "I'm Dr. Rose. I understand you're having some pain in your back, Mr..." There seemed to be no point in engaging the man on her gender, though she was still somewhat surprised that people were surprised.

"Moses," the man said, biting off the word clearly and with apparent pride.

Sylvia nodded, not really paying attention. There were forty thousand Mexicans in Denver, though the man didn't look Hispanic. "Moses what?"

The man's wife was with him, a short, dark woman who was clearly embarrassed by her husband's truculence. Sylvia understood and wanted to reassure her. She knew people were often frustrated by the refusal of their bodies to function properly, as if illness indicated some failure of character rather than biological fact. "It's all right," Sylvia said, patting the woman's shoulder. Then, to the man, speaking slowly, as if he hadn't understood her the first time. "I need your surname, your last name, please?"

This only seemed to anger the patient further. "I know what surname means," he said. "I'm an educated man, an engineer. Don't patronize me." Then, "That's it."

Sylvia was confused. It was late and her husband was out of town at a stamp convention in San Diego, which created new problems in her day. She had to pick up the kids at the sitter's at five and it was already 4:15. It would be nice if she could call and simply tell them she had been delayed, but she knew from experience that all they would understand from this was that their mother was late, again, and she hated that, hated failing them. Now she shook her head, wondering if she had missed something, feeling for the hundredth time that day that she was doing too much and doing it all inadequately. Still, it was important to remain professional. She took a deep breath. "What?" she asked. "What's it?"

The man seemed to glow with pride, actually to become taller. "My name. Moses. That's all there is; I have no last name."

"Ah," Sylvia said. Now she understood. The man was delusional. Of course the intake clerk hadn't asked for a psychiatric consult because the presenting problem was back pain and there were no psychiatrists on staff since psychiatry had been carved out last month. Besides, even if there were a psychiatrist on call what would be the point in initiating therapy with someone who thought he was about to lead the Israelites down into Egypt? Medication might be indicated, but she could do that. Her main problem now was trying to figure out if this man posed a danger to himself or to his wife, if he was too crazy to continue among the general population.

Sylvia took a deep breath and smiled at the couple. "Well, then," she said, "Why don't you tell me how you hurt your back, Mr. Moses?"

The man patted two large ledgers which Sylvia now noticed sat next to him on the examining table. "I was carrying these down the mountain, and I fell. But that's not important. What's important is that I get the Word to President Obama as soon as possible. Seconds count, you know. World peace is at stake."

Sylvia remembered from her psychiatry rotation in medical school that it was important not to interrupt the psychosis, but rather to try to enter into it and discover the internal logic, if there was one. Yet she found it hard to reconcile the man's diction and scholarly manner with what he was saying and his wife looked terrified. Whatever might be going on with his back, it was becoming clear that the patient needed to be in another setting, preferably in a hospital. "Maybe I should take a look at your books in my office for a moment and then we can decide what to do," Sylvia suggested, picking up one of the ledgers.

Outside, she asked the intake clerk where the man had come from. "He was sitting in the middle of the street, tying up traffic on Colorado Boulevard," the woman said. "He told the cops he couldn't move because of his back. The paramedics brought him here when they figured out he had insurance."

It was absurd but made a kind of sense in the new world of medicine. Bring a delusional patient to a managed care clinic rather than the general hospital which was equipped to handle people like this. Why? Because unlike the other psychotics wandering the streets at any time of the night or day he had insurance. The diabolical part was Sylvia knew that if this Moses was allowed to start here, he would be the clinic's responsibility until he was released. Unless they could immediately send him to another facility. "So then you called me," Sylvia said.

"You're the neurologist. It was his back. That's what he said."

"His back?" Sylvia said, incredulous. "The man's out of his mind. He thinks he's Moses carrying the word of God to an anxious world."

The clerk was chewing gum and rolling her hair into curls with a red pencil. Sylvia thought she might be twenty-one. "He said his back hurt," the girl said, pouting now. "How do I know if he's crazy or not? Lots of Mexicans named Moses."

Sylvia could see there was no point in arguing. "This guy's problem is a lot farther up than his back," she said. "I'm calling the police."

"You're going to arrest him?"

"No, the police will. What I'm going to do is put him on a mental health hold. The police will take him over to Denver Health and then he'll be in an appropriate place, at least for 72 hours. After that, we'll see. Probably depends on how good his insurance is. They can also take care of his back at the hospital."

And that was all there was to it, at least as far as Sylvia was concerned. The patient was carrying the word of God to the Leader of the Free World but she had to get him out of her clinic. Simple. She had transferred Moses' care to a psychiatrist she knew slightly who covered the wards at Denver Health. After a brief volley of voice-mail messages back and forth, she forgot about it. Until now.

Until she received the blue letter from the medical committee at the hospital requiring her presence at a Mortality and Morbidity hearing. The Moses had apparently tried to kill himself with a bed sheet in the locked ward at the hospital and Sylvia had been listed as his physician. Which was ridiculous; she told herself it was all a mistake.

Still, she was required to attend the hearing and Mitchell was out of town, again. Someone was opening a new store in Salt Lake City and his company was having a trunk sale to bring in customers. It was essential that Mitchell be there, he said. This was the way her husband thought. He projected a kind of sincerity that she found touching, even convincing and she wanted to be supportive of his work. Recently, however, she found that rather than missing Mitchell when he was gone, she was glad to have the time to herself. She could eat what she liked, go to bed when she wanted and get up whenever it suited her. Not that Mitchell made many demands but she found she liked the fact that he wasn't there, that she didn't have to think about him and could focus instead on her work and the kids.

Sylvia called a friend who agreed to get Simon and Becky at school. "This shouldn't take too long," she said, speaking with more confidence than she felt about the M&M. Doctors weren't known for their efficiency in these matters. It wasn't likely to be any different today.

The meeting was held in a windowless conference room. Someone had installed color-coordinated pads on the walls in an effort at sound-proofing. A large tape recorder sat in the middle of the table and a man with earphones was fiddling with the dials when Sylvia came in. Seated behind the table were Joe Steffes, the chief of medicine, Herman Goldensohn, an older doctor she didn't know who ran the outpatient unit, and two nurses. All of which was unusual since normally the doctors conducting the M&M would be specialists rather than administrators or section heads. Sylvia reminded herself that she hadn't really treated Moses, and certainly not for a neurological ailment. Still, it was strange.

Sylvia had known Steffes since medical school. He had been Head Resident when she was a third year student and was a favorite with the house staff, but they'd had no contact in years. He looked gray and middle-aged now, borne down by his responsibilities, she supposed. She wondered if she had changed similarly, but even if she had her looks weren't the point today. Joe greeted Sylvia warmly and said, "This isn't really an investigation, you know. More of a conversation about a very unfortunate accident."

Steffes' diction made her wary. She distrusted the warm and friendly approach but it wouldn't do to start out in a suspicious frame of mind. Besides, Sylvia approved of investigating patients' deaths or attempted suicides even if it could be inconvenient or embarrassing for the physician involved. Every service at the hospital conducted M&Ms, though most would be more technical than this one. She had attended oncology M&Ms that included the examination of slides of diseased tissue and abstruse discussions of experimental surgical procedures. Cure rates. Percentages. This was going to be different because Moses was.

Once they were seated, she asked, "What am I doing here, Joe?"

This seemed to catch Steffes off-balance. He was supposed to ask the questions, but his colleague saved him. Tall and saturnine with an acquired eastern accent, Herman Goldensohn looked over his glasses and said, "A man has tried to kill himself, Sylvia. That is why we are here. It's a very serious matter. I should think that would be obvious."

Sylvia hardly knew Goldensohn and resented the older man's patronizing her, but she controlled her anger. "I understand the reason for the M&M, Doctor," she said, "and I realize it's serious, but that wasn't my question. I asked what I was doing here. I'm not his doctor. I wasn't following him and only saw him once, at the clinic. I do have privileges here but I'm not at the hospital very often and I communicated with the psychiatrist on call before calling the police and sending the patient over. That's the procedure we use. More to the point, though, as I asked before, how am I involved in this at all?"

Steffes shuffled through a pile of papers on the table before him and finally came to the one he had been looking for. He held it up and examined it closely. Then, anxious to regain control of the meeting, his voice took on a more formal tone. "This man, Robert Mankwitz, was referred here by you, isn't that correct, Sylvia? Didn't you sign these orders?" He held up the paper.

Sylvia felt tired. She remembered reading somewhere that repetition was a method of interrogation, effective in breaking down potential terrorists. Just keep asking the same question over and over and at some point they'd collapse and reveal important things. She didn't know if Goldensohn was trying to break her down or just had bad short-term memory. She wondered what his kids were doing, if they'd been picked up on time and who drove them to their lessons and doctors' appointments. She was conscious as she was so often of where she should be right now, of what she should be doing. She wondered if these men ever thought of their children during the course of the day, of whether they had eaten lunch or had a good day at school. She doubted they ever worried about the mundane details of life that clogged her every waking moment. No doubt they left those things to their wives, sensible women who didn't collect stamps or work outside the home.

"Of course I sent him over. I just told you that. But I only saw him that one time, six weeks ago, in the clinic. The police brought him in because he sat down in the middle of Colorado Boulevard and was a public nuisance. The only reason I examined him at all was that he was complaining of back pain, which made him a neurological case. Then when I met him and his wife, Mr. Mankwitz introduced himself as Moses, no last name, bearer of the word of God. He said he had hurt his back coming down from Mt. Sinai."

"We are aware of the facts of the case," Goldensohn said, his voice echoing in the room. "We know that Mr. Mankwitz was a deeply troubled man and quite confused when you saw him."

"Confused?" Sylvia laughed. "Oh, no, Doctor, he wasn't confused. He was floridly psychotic. He should never have been taken to my clinic in the first place. It wasn't safe for him or anyone else to have him there. This is why I put him on a hold and sent him here, where Bill Olson could take care of him, as he told me he would. My question is why aren't you talking to Bill?"

Steffes ignored this and continued to read silently. Then he looked up at Sylvia. "It says he was released two days later, Sylvia. There isn't much about what went on during those two days, but according to the process report, both you and Dr. Olson assented to his release."

Sylvia shook her head. This was getting more bizarre by the moment. If Mankwitz had been released, why were they even talking about it? The man must have been re-admitted at a later time, but, if so, that had even less to do with her. "It was a formality," Sylvia said. "I didn't even talk to Bill about the case. The charge-nurse told me they had loaded Mr.Mankwitz up with Haldol and Depakote and that he had calmed down enough to go home. That would have been Bill's decision because he was the attending on the unit. There would have been no reason for me to question his judgment since I hadn't even seen the patient."

Goldensohn held his copy of the paper close to his face and read silently for a few minutes. She couldn't believe these guys. You'd think they would have read the process notes before holding the meeting, but as far as she could tell this was all new to them. "According to the report, you never met with Dr. Olson or with Mr. Mankwitz after he was admitted to the hospital," Goldensohn said. He placed his glasses carefully on the table and looked at her significantly. "Never convened a family conference? Surely you wouldn't take the word of a nurse in a situation like this, would you, Doctor Rose?"

The nurses present seemed to stiffen at this, but Goldensohn didn't deign to notice them. "Sure, I would," Sylvia said. "I do it all the time because it's good medicine. The nurses are on the ward and we're not. They're with the patients all day and they have a much better sense of what's going on than the doctors do. We only see patients when we make rounds. We even give our orders over the phone. If there's a problem or the patient needs a change in his medication, the nurses will call. And even if Olson and I didn't meet, we both agreed with the nurse's assessment. Based on their observations, I saw no problem in letting the patient go home. I doubt that any physician in Denver would have done anything different. Anyway, if Mankwitz was released, how did he get back into the hospital to try to kill himself?"

Steffes looked back at his papers. "His wife apparently brought him to the emergency room several weeks later saying he had threatened her. Assuming he would be a risk to the other patients, the night attending physician ordered him put in the locked ward and he was left unattended long enough to find a way to try to hang himself. The note from the ED lists you as his doctor."

That explained why they hadn't called Bill Olson. "Well, that's obviously a mistake," Sylvia said. "Probably they checked his chart from the previous admission and went from there. But if they thought I was his doctor, I wonder why no one called me when they admitted him," Sylvia said. "Shouldn't they have checked with me before doing anything with the patient?"

"I can't answer that," Steffes said. "Perhaps they tried or maybe they assumed you'd be rounding in the morning." He looked at the report again. "He was admitted at 3:45 AM. Someone in the ED may have made a mistake." He shrugged and pushed his hand through his hair in a boyish gesture. So that's how it happened, she thought. People working under pressure, mad with distraction. Someone made a mistake. She was listed as Mankwitz' doctor on some form and everything flowed from that one error. It was a busy hospital and everyone was over-worked. Steffes made no apologies for that and Sylvia didn't disagree with him, even if the result had been a failed suicide attempt.

"Going back to your examination," Goldensohn said, breaking the collegial atmosphere. "I assume that when you saw him, you asked Mr. Mankwitz if he was thinking about suicide."

The inquisitional tone was getting to her. She didn't know what Steffes was after but Goldensohn was obviously determined to hold her feet to the fire. Sylvia was equally determined not to lose her composure but the older doctor was making it hard. "Of course," she said. "It made him laugh. After all, he had just been to Mount Sinai to pick up those tablets he was carrying and he was on his way to the White House with crucial instructions for the President. Looking at it from his point of view, it would have been a hell of a time to kill himself."

Goldensohn didn't respond to her sarcasm. "Did you ask if he'd been eating and sleeping, whether he was on medication?"

Sylvia just looked at the other doctors in amazement. Were they serious? These were questions any medical student would know enough to ask and it was all covered in the patient's chart. "Of course I did," she said. "The intake clerk also verified his insurance."

Goldensohn perked up at this, apparently suspecting he might have caught Sylvia in a crucial mistake. "So in addition to consulting nurses, you allowed an insurance company to influence your treatment of the patient?"

"Who doesn't?" Sylvia asked. "What choice do we have anymore? Could you honestly tell me he would have been admitted to the hospital without someone asking about it?"

Which was true, but not really the point and Sylvia felt instantly ashamed of herself for defending herself on a technicality. The more important truth was that none of them, neither she nor Bill Olson nor any of the ED doctors or nurses had evinced any real concern for this befuddled man who on a crazily busy day like a thousand others had received routine treatment before being loaded up with drugs and sent home with the hope that nothing awful would happen. Now that she wasn't trying to treat Mankwitz, Sylvia could feel empathy for him rather than annoyance. She could also admit privately that if on that afternoon she had more time, more patience, and more support, she might have sat and listened to his theories at length instead of going into the next room and calling the police.

But this was not life as she lived it day in and day out in the less than ideal medical world in which she functioned. There was never enough time to do all she should do. Sylvia did the best she could. Now she understood belatedly that this wasn't really a fact-finding hearing at all. Nor really a search for a medical misstep that might have caused a patient to attempt suicide. None of that. The essential point of this hearing was to shift liability for Mankwitz' misfortune from the hospital to her. This was why they were interrogating her rather than Bill Olson. Bill represented the hospital while Sylvia was an independent contractor whom the hospital didn't cover under their general malpractice policy.

Beyond this, there was no real reason for an M&M because there was little to investigate. The facts of the case spoke for themselves. An out-of-work psychotic patient had tried to kill himself. She thought wryly the true miracle was that such things didn't happen more often. Medicine the helping profession and she the caregiver. Why so often did they neither help nor care? Everyone in the room knew this, just as they knew that Sylvia was a competent doctor, better than most, that she did good work, and missed very little.

Sylvia turned to Steffes. "Is there a complaint against me, Bob? Because if there isn't, I'm going to leave. I've still got notes to write and then I have to pick up my kids at school."

Steffes sighed and turned to Goldensohn who leaned over and cupped his hand to the other man's ear. Steffes nodded, then turned to Sylvia. "I'm sorry," he said, and this time Sylvia sensed that he really was. "But Mr. Mankwitz has hired an attorney and they've filed a complaint. I don't think this is going anywhere, but it's our responsibility as officers of the hospital to look at it."

Now everything made sense. It was a legal matter. Liability not medicine was at issue. "What's the complaint, then? Is Olson being sued too?"

Steffes shook his head. "Since Mr. Mankwitz and his wife considered you to be their doctor, you're the only one mentioned. Originally they'd forgotten your name and just referred to you as the Jewish doctor he saw at the clinic."

"I'm certainly not the only Jewish physician in town or even the only one with privileges at the hospital."

Steffes blushed, embarrassed. "Of course not, but you were the one who signed the original hold on Mr. Mankwitz before Dr. Olson picked him up in the hospital."

It made Sylvia feel the slightest bit guilty that Mankwitz had identified with her as a member of the tribe. No doubt he felt doubly mistreated that a fellow Jew had sent him off to a holding pen rather than showing concern. And thus the lawsuit. Religion aside, however, Sylvia still believed she had done nothing wrong. "But Bill agreed with me. It's right there in front of you."

Steffes ran his fingers through his hair and straightened his tie, obviously uncomfortable, but Goldensohn stepped in again, his voice harsh in the small room. "Be that as it may, it's no excuse for your inattention."

There was no point in arguing because it had gone beyond that now. Sylvia didn't like the way she had been treated but she didn't really blame the two men. The hospital had a lot more to lose potentially than she did. Steffes and Goldensohn were just covering their asses. She shivered in the room, though it was warmer than she would ordinarily have liked. Just once she wished someone would exceed her expectations and show a little class.

She was perpetually disappointed with the men in her life even if she knew it had little to do with the fact that they were men. If it came down to it, it was scary too, because this was her livelihood, her lifeline, the key to her independence of Mitchell's family fortune. This realization, irrelevant as it was to the M&M, made her furious that once again her husband was gone at a critical moment.

Anger was a luxury, however, and the fact that now there was a complaint against her that she'd have to read thoroughly and answer did little to change the reality of her life, which was that the kids needed to be picked up at the sitter's. "Can I see that?" Sylvia said, pointing at the papers Steffes was holding. "The complaint, I mean."

Steffes slid a bound report across the table. "I guess you'll have to respond in writing," he said.

Sylvia glanced at the complaint then hefted it in her hand. Someone had taken a lot of care with this. It had been typed on bond, single-spaced with numerous strikeovers. "It looks like a book," she said.

Steffes smiled ruefully. "Fifty-four pages, with notes and an index," he said. "Good luck."

Sylvia had no time to read Mankwitz' complaint or even think much about it until she had called for the children, fed them and sat with them while they did their homework. Then she fell asleep reading his description of her as an egregiously incompetent practitioner with an unnatural interest in money and a corresponding lack of empathy for patients.

The next day Mitchell returned from Utah and after putting the children to bed, Sylvia listened to his description of his trip. She envied Mitchell his total absorption in something that virtually no one else cared about. It was in its own way a gift, a certain sort of confidence. She knew it might be said of all great men that they were self-absorbed but no one would ever have called Mitchell a great man. He wasn't even important to his company, having a sinecure because of family connections. Yet there was still a part of Sylvia that regarded Mitchell with admiration for his enthusiasm for what he did. More than admire, she envied him and often wished she had a fraction of his self- regard for what she did.

"That's great," Sylvia said, trying to show more enthusiasm than she felt. She wasn't sure if she loved Mitchell or had ever loved him but she knew some women would consider her to be fortunate. By the standards of the community, he was a good husband. He had a job, he didn't drink, and he participated in childcare and household chores with an energy she sometimes found exhausting. As far as she knew he was faithful. Still, when she looked at him in the light of the small family room, the golden reflection of the lamp playing on his pink scalp, she felt sad. They weren't old, just barely into middle age, but she felt that their lives reflected little sense of a wider world, although the talk that evening might be of classical music and the theater.

At first, she had resisted what she knew she felt about Mitchell and their marriage, blaming her boredom on exhaustion and a busy schedule. But over time she had come to accept the truth: that it was unsatisfying to talk with her husband about her work, that she didn't look forward to seeing him, and that she didn't mind his periodic absences. She had been raised to respect culture and involvement in the Jewish community, but she found Mitchell ponderous. And while they both thought of themselves as being cultured, she couldn't remember their last political discussion or a book they had both enjoyed. Their conversations sketched the quotidian: who was free when to take the kids from here to there; who would shop for groceries; who would cook. It was necessary, she knew, but somehow soul-destroying. As time went by, she had begun to feel panicky about life getting away from her. This wasn't Mitchell's fault, of course, but she associated it with him, and thought of her marriage as being similar to a long and chronic illness.

At a conference, Sylvia had heard a woman describe a divorce study she conducted focused on women with what she called "starter-husbands," nice men who would share the housework, give their wives space, and were neither threatened by their success nor threatening themselves. Unfortunately, these men were seldom exciting either, and in the psychologist's study, all of her subjects eventually left their husbands once they were established in their professions. Sylvia wondered if this would be her destiny. Whatever fault she might find with Mitchell, she no longer saw herself in a very attractive light either. She was still slim and reasonably young, but she envied women who were regulars at health clubs, took Pilates and had spa days with friends.

It made her feel guilty to think that in some manner she might have unconsciously used Mitchell as a convenient way to realize her goals of having children and finishing medical school on time. But that didn't make it easier to live with him. Sometimes it seemed that there was insufficient air to breathe.

Whether Mitchell suspected any of this was a mystery. He possessed an odd self-satisfaction that despite herself she liked. Once, at a party, he had been challenged by a drunk who said businessmen were parasites living off the sweat of the people and contributed nothing to society. Mitchell listened to the man patiently then remarked that he was living the life he wanted to live. Sylvia thought at the time that few people she knew could say that.

Originally, their interests seemed much the same, but when Sylvia left graduate school to study medicine, Mitchell had been supportive but puzzled by her interest in neurology. "It takes so much time," he had said, "and you'll be surrounded by so many sad people who can't be helped."

Tonight, she said, "I'm getting sued."

"Uh, huh," Mitchell said, as if it had nothing to do with him. "What about?"

His detachment irritated her. He acted as if they were talking about someone else or something he had read in the paper. But if she were sued, they'd all be affected. She'd have to hire a lawyer and immerse herself in the minutiae of her defense. This wasn't a minor consideration; it could change their lives. So why didn't he react? She waited but Mitchell said nothing further. Finally, she answered the question. "A man who thinks he's Moses complained about me. I had to go to an M&M."

Mitchell nodded seriously. "Interesting," he said. He put his book down and looked thoughtful. "I suppose in some small way we're all Moses, all delivering divine messages from on high. It's an interesting conceit, perhaps a different way of looking at the world and our missions within it. What sort of man was this?"

This reaction was so far from Sylvia's concerns that she didn't know how to respond. She felt like laughing, but then anger washed in behind the humor and she wanted to brain her husband. He was sitting faced away from her. She remembered a scene in a Conrad novel she had read in graduate school. A misunderstood wife kills her husband with a large knife when he mistakenly imagines she was in the mood for love. Sylvia hadn't understood it then, but she did now.

An M&M was not a philosophical inquiry and the word of god wasn't a metaphor to Mankwitz; he actually thought he *was* Moses. But even that didn't get to the heart of it. Sylvia was scared. Months after she had seen Mankwitz in the clinic, he had gone to the trouble to write an incredible document detailing his grievances with no regard for the truth. What if he came after her somehow, or after the kids? Did he know where her office was, where she lived? What real security did she have? The hospital administrators wanted to protect themselves and seemed to think she was culpable in some way. Yet Mitchell seemed unconcerned.

"Did you know that some people lose their licenses over things like this?" She was over-stating the situation, and she knew it, trying to get a rise out of her husband. In all likelihood, the case would be dismissed and it was out of the question that she would lose her license. She wanted Mitchell's support yet unable to ask directly, she wanted him to know instinctively what she needed. It was about more than losing her income; having been raised in a wealthy family, Mitchell never worried about money or questioned his right to a patrician existence.

"This doesn't bother you?" she continued. "You don't think it's just slightly worrisome to have someone petitioning the State Board over my treatment of him and demanding they take action?"

Mitchell removed his wire-rimmed spectacles and polished them on his shirttail before replacing them. "We live in a litigious age," he said mildly. "Law suits have taken the place of angry phone calls for many people, I guess."

Once more Sylvia remembered Conrad. If I don't leave this man I will suffocate, she thought, surprising herself with her vehemence. "Yes," she said, her voice heavy with sarcasm. "I guess it's just a very common thing these days."

Mitchell cleared his throat. "A friend of mine from college is up on charges for complimenting a woman who works for him on her hairstyle," he said. "Sexual harassment."

"I hope she wins," Sylvia said and left the room.

When she finally worked her way through Mankwitz' screed, Sylvia found it oddly comforting. While he did accuse her of incompetence he seemed to put more emphasis on her avarice and skepticism. Her treatment of his injury never came up. It bothered him that she didn't believe his story: it was clear to him that she doubted that he'd been to the mountain top and was in direct contact with the Lord. He said this was what had landed him in the psychiatric ward. Rather than taking his mission seriously, she called the police, and this had only compounded the problems Mankwitz admitted he had, though losing his job had not been his fault. In fact, he suggested in the text that Sylvia was in cahoots with his former supervisor, an anti Semite named O'Connor who was unwilling to grant him time off for his pilgrimage.

Everything followed logically from that. The suicide attempt grew out of Mankwitz' feelings of despair at having failed to get God's message of peace to the world. Sylvia read all this with open-mouthed wonder. Bob Steffes might be nervous, but Sylvia knew that no investigatory body was going to sanction her for believing that a man who presented himself as Moses had psychiatric problems.

She saw the button glow on her telephone and picked up. "Dr. Rose?" She recognized Thomas Morris' voice and felt her heart skip. This irritated her so she took a more formal tone than she might have otherwise.

This is Dr. Rose," she said in a neutral tone.

Thomas didn't identify himself but merely plunged forward. "I'm sorry to bother you. But you've got to help me. They won't give me my medicine," he said, his voice hurried in her ear.

"What do you mean?" Sylvia said. She was still thinking of Mankwitz, Jehovah and Mt. Sinai.

"That new medicine you prescribed. They said they don't approve of it, it's not the right formula or something."

"Formulary," Sylvia corrected him. Every managed care company had lists of drugs they would approve and those they would not, depending generally less on their efficacy in treating patients than the terms they could negotiate with the drug companies. What concerned Sylvia more than the formulary was that Thomas didn't seem stable. While she hadn't arrived at a firm diagnosis, she was working on the assumption that Thomas was suffering from Lupus. There were essentially two kinds of the disease, one relatively benign and the other more aggressive. Thomas had started with fairly mild symptoms, but it wasn't unusual for patients to crash after six months or so and that's what seemed to be happening now.

Given the options, Sylvia had decided medication was the only practical treatment. The problem was what to prescribe. Steroids were anti-inflammatories and could control pain and acute symptoms but they did nothing to blunt the inevitable progression of the disease, so she had decided to try another drug she had read about recently, a powerful immunosuppressant. She took a deep breath. Moses would have to wait. "Let me give them a call," she said to Thomas. "Try not to worry too much. I'll get back to you."

When she finally reached the case manager late that afternoon, however, she ran into a brick wall. "We consider Cellcept to be an experimental drug, Doctor," the woman said. "We don't authorize it for treatment of lupus."

"And it's very expensive," Sylvia said, trying not to sound too annoyed.

"That's true too," the case manager said. "Have you tried Prednisone? That is on our formulary and we've had good results with that with some other patients."

This was true but Sylvia also knew that long-term steroid use often led to heart disease or aseptic necrosis. In other words, Prednisone might be effective but in this case the cure could be as bad as the disease.

"I'm sure that's a serious consideration for everyone," the case manager said now, "even if they're not famous musicians."

And she was right. It was Sylvia's bias.

There was a silence on the phone and Sylvia wondered if the case manager was thinking it over, if possibly she was getting somewhere at last. "I guess I could authorize a trial," she said slowly.

Sylvia was quiet, afraid she'd say the wrong thing.

"I'll give you six weeks on the Cellcept," the case worker said now. "We'll re-evaluate it then." And before Sylvia could express gratitude or surprise, she said, "You have a nice day now," and was gone.

Sylvia got a call from Bob Steffes later in the week to tell her the complaint against her had been resolved and there would be no lawsuit. "I'm sorry we had to put you through that," he said.

"You didn't," Sylvia replied. Steffes was a decent man but she resented the show of force he and Goldensohn had presented at the M&M. "I never should have been in that room. I wasn't Mankwitz' doctor and you might have had some faith in my work instead of accepting the word of a lunatic."

"We thought you were his doctor," Steffes said. "You were the one named in the complaint. Regardless of Mr. Mankwitz' competence, we had to follow up."

"You needed to cover your ass, you mean?" Sylvia's anger surprised her, but Steffes didn't rise to the bait.

"Something like that," he admitted. "No hard feelings, I hope?"

"Not as long as you admit it," Sylvia said. And it was true. Sometimes she wished she were better at holding a grudge, but forgiveness was one of her weaknesses. Steffes was neither better nor worse than other administrators, but in questions of legal liability, no one wanted to be responsible, or admit that sometimes mistakes were made by good people. Hospitals and insurance companies fell all over themselves in their rush to disclaim responsibility, which left doctors with few choices. Sylvia felt sometimes as if she had a target printed on the back of her white coat. Still, she knew part of the problem grew out of her own willingness to believe she had done something wrong, missed something, whether she had or not. Still, she neither wanted nor expected sympathy from Steffes. She hung up feeling unfulfilled.

The following week she was back at the clinic seeing patients when she looked up to see Mrs. Mankwitz standing in her office door. She was wearing a blue-flowered housedress and carried a tan knapsack. "Can I come in?" she asked.

The terrified wife. Sylvia felt sorry for anyone with the misfortune to be married to Mankwitz but this wasn't really a time for sympathy. "I'm sorry, but I shouldn't be talking to you," Sylvia said. "Your husband is suing me."

"Oh, Bob didn't mean anything by that," Mrs. Mankwitz said quickly, and despite herself Sylvia smiled. The woman was just like Mitchell. She treated a lawsuit like a fraternity prank. Spraying windows with paint. Parking a car on top of a building.

"I'm afraid he did," Sylvia said gently. "The hospital administrators certainly thought so."

"Really," Mrs. Mankwitz said. "Our neighbor is a lawyer and he's the one who convinced Bob to do it. He's about the least legal person I know." Now she came into the room and grasped Sylvia's hand. "I'm really sorry, but anyway I'm worried about my husband."

Sylvia couldn't blame the woman, but it seemed ironic that she would be the person Mrs. Mankwitz would call in her hour of need. "I really don't see how I can help," she said.

"But you're our only hope," Mrs. Mankwitz wailed.

"Our?" Sylvia said.

The woman nodded vigorously. "Bob's the one who asked me to come."

Sylvia had limited sympathy for the man but it wasn't his wife's fault. Patients with appointments were waiting outside and she wasn't a social worker. She sighed and put down her hand. "Okay, Mrs. Mankwitz, how do you think I can help?" For in the end, that was the only question. She was a doctor; she had been trained to help people. It was what she was supposed to do.

"I don't know," Mrs. Mankwitz said. "He just seems like a wild man, tearing around the house. He doesn't sleep, he's always writing in those books. I'm afraid he's going off again like he did before, when we came to see you."

"Are you worried about your safety?" Sylvia asked. "I know an excellent shelter I could refer you to." It was what Sylvia would have wanted.

"It's not that. Bob'd never hurt me. I'm worried about him hurting himself, like he did in the hospital. I was just wondering if I could get him down here, if you'd talk to him."

"I'm the last person he'd listen to," Sylvia said.

"Oh, no," Mrs. Mankwitz said. "That was all a mistake. Honestly. He admires you, talks about you all the time. He wants to explain everything but he's afraid you're mad at him so he sent me instead."

Sylvia had to laugh. "Admires me? For what?" She wasn't fishing for compliments. She really couldn't see how the man who'd written the complaint could also think well of her.

Now Mrs. Mankwitz looked surprised. "You kidding? You've got everything. You're young, pretty, smart, you've got a good job. You're a doctor so everyone looks up to you." She glanced at Sylvia's family pictures on the bureau. "Even a husband and kids. Who wouldn't look up to you?"

Sylvia surveyed the cluttered office. Papers cascaded from the desk, medical journals littered the floor, books were jammed into the shelves at odd angles. And while she adored her children, she would have considered her marriage a model for no one. She knew that her problems were nothing when she thought of her patients struggling with incurable illnesses, but they occupied her waking and sleeping hours nevertheless. "Well, if you really think it would help, I'll talk to your husband," Sylvia said, wondering if this was a good idea.

A sweet smile bordered by dimples transformed the woman's face. She came around the desk and threw her arms around Sylvia. "Oh, thank you," she said. "Thank you so much."

Mrs. Mankwitz was wearing cologne, too much of it. Violets, Sylvia thought. But it had been a long time since she had felt so sincerely appreciated and now she realized that she had missed this, that it was the reason she had become a doctor in the first place. She had been young and idealistic then but in this particular way nothing had changed. She wanted to help people but she also wanted them to express their gratitude. It seemed ignoble but it was the truth.

Standing in the small office, locked in Mrs. Mankwitz' hot embrace, Sylvia smelled the cheap perfume and thought of lost ideals, failed marriages, and the unexpected rewards of service. The fascination of any life but certainly hers lay in its utter unpredictability. What mattered at this moment was that her patient needed her. That was the reality, her reality. Regardless of what had happened in the past, she would do what she could when Mankwitz came back to her office.

CHAPTER THREE

Since that first interview with Thomas Morris, Sylvia had thought of him fleetingly if at all. She had ten other patients on her schedule that day and every other day, not to mention rounding at the hospital and meeting with the interns from the university whom she supervised. There was a Darwinian self-selection process that went on the last year of medical school when students chose their specialties. Some of the smartest students went into neurology but usually not the most caring ones. Generally, the problems of neurological patients were chronic or fatal. A fellow student had put it succinctly: "They never get well."

After running a series of tests and consulting with one of her former professors at the medical school to confirm her diagnosis, Sylvia had her secretary call Thomas to schedule an appointment. And now he was here, waiting in her outer office. She felt nervous, like a girl waiting for a date. She looked around the room and suppressed a wild impulse to tidy up or clear space on the available sofa. Then she decided what was good for other patients had to be good enough for Thomas and his wife.

The intercom came alive again. "Doctor?" the secretary questioned, as if somehow Sylvia had gone out. She smiled to herself and braced herself for the day. "Coming right now," she said.

She could have seen Thomas in an examining room rather than her office, but she'd already examined him so what would be the point?

When they were all seated, she put his chart on the desk and said, "I'm afraid you have lupus erythematosus, Mr. Morris. I'm sorry." She found it best to be simple and straightforward about these things, just say the words, get it out there, whatever it might be. But she knew this case had the potential to involve her emotionally so to protect herself her voice more clipped than usual. Thomas should really be seeing a rheumatologist, but in their wisdom the administrators of the insurance company had decided in the lexicon of managed care to "carve out" rheumatology and assign all such cases to an outside practice. Gatekeepers didn't like to use outsiders because it cost them more money. Sylvia had won a prize in rheumatology in medical school and Thomas had presented with dizziness originally, so assigning his case to a neurologist made sense to the case managers, whether it was the best care for the patient or not.

Now, Thomas looked impressed. He fingered his face gently and looked at Sylvia. "What about this?" he asked. "I didn't know lupus was a skin disease." He sat up straighter in his seat, glowing with interest in this new thing, this disease. He was pleased that Sylvia had put a name to his condition so quickly when it had perplexed his other doctors.

Sylvia reached over and touched his cheek lightly, his flesh cool against her warm fingers. "It's not really a dermatological condition," she said. "What you have is called a malar rash. It's often the first sign of lupus. Classic. The red mask makes you look like a wolf which is what lupus erythematosus means. Red wolf."

"So you knew from the beginning," Thomas said. "But if it's so obvious, why didn't any of those other bozos figure it out?" Sylvia didn't treat many artists, but she was struck by Thomas Morris' need to be unusual. If he must be sick, he needed to be special. His condition should be resistant to diagnosis, requiring teams of specialists, a battery of tests, and perhaps a visit to a world-renowned medical center in order to arrive at an answer. It should be more puzzling, even bizarre. He would have wanted his to be an orphan case, one in a million, to be written up in a medical journal. The fact that his symptoms were classic deflated him. Jaunty when he came in, he now slumped in his chair, depressed.

Sylvia would have considered it inappropriate to tell him illness was always interesting to a physician because each patient was unique and responded differently. Yet what seemed oddest about Thomas' reaction was the apparent absence of a tragic sense, the growing realization that life would now change dramatically and never be the same for him again. Television appeals for funds gave the lie to the notion that a cure for cancer, multiple sclerosis, rheumatoid arthritis or anything else was just around the corner if people would only walk, run, bike and, most important, give money to the cause.

"I needed to confirm my initial impression," Sylvia said. "Without clinical confirmation, your insurance company wouldn't authorize a treatment plan."

This seemed to mean nothing to Thomas. Despite his mood, however, his attitude toward Sylvia hadn't changed. He was flattering in his attention to what she said, even slightly flirtatious. She didn't mind. She didn't feel threatened by a patient with a potentially fatal disease. Sick or not she admired him and his accomplishments.

She went through her notes again, nodding her head as if in agreement with something clever she had said. "More music is going to be a problem. It depends in part on how much you have to travel." She thought his career as a concert artist was probably over but there was no point in telling him so soon after giving him his diagnosis. Better to let him discover the limitations on his own.

"How bad will it be?" Thomas asked.

His directness surprised her, especially since this was the most difficult question to answer. Doctors usually said every patient was different, which was both true and evasive. Physicians wanted to protect themselves, especially given the possibility for error. And even if Thomas said he wanted to know the truth, it was unlikely that he'd really be anxious to hear the gruesome details: that he would be lucky to avoid paralysis and total bed rest, and sooner rather than later.

Sylvia wondered if in a part of herself she was still defending against her sense of him. As if it was her diagnosis rather than the disease that was responsible for ending a brilliant career. She straightened in her chair, and took a middle ground, "Lupus is generally progressive, but there are cases in which people live comfortably for years."

"And then they die?" Thomas asked, a wistful smile on his face.

"Everybody dies," Sylvia said, aware again that she wanted to reassure him and make him feel better even if there was no way to feel very good about this.

Thomas nodded. "It's odd," he said. "But I don't find all this particularly discouraging."

She liked his precise way of speaking, his diction. Acknowledging that the disease was not good news he seemed to suggest that other things might have been worse.

"I'm sorry to have to tell you this," Sylvia said, and she was.

Thomas nodded, but he still seemed more thoughtful than sad. "I had just always assumed that I would go on as I had, you know, playing concerts, slowly, building a better career. Become more widely-known, maybe make some interesting recordings. It's funny but music makes you humble. All of us are unbearably arrogant, but we know exactly where we fit in the pecking order, who's better, who's younger, who's the new exciting player." He hesitated now, parsing his words carefully and nodding his head as at an emerging truth.

"I see it all very differently now, life, the future. Whatever I had in the way of talent was temporary, like a loan, and the disease has called it in. Music, performing, that's all over for me. You're not really saying that but we both know it's true. The funny thing is that it seems incredibly unimportant and yet it's what I've dedicated my life to until now."

Sylvia nodded sympathetically. Thomas might be a concert artist but, like most patients, he had spent his life in denial. Serious illness always happened to someone else. Doctors were no different, defending against reality by making mordant jokes. She remembered long nights in the Emergency Room when they'd announce the death of patient by saying that so-and-so had checked out or had his ticket punched.

Not knowing what else to do or say, Sylvia reached across the desk and placed her hand on his. "Call whenever you want," she said. She wrote her home telephone number on her card and handed it to him. "I know this won't be easy."

Constantly traveling from her home in Southeast Denver downtown to the hospital and then back to the clinic, Sylvia had come to think of her car as an extension of herself, not her home exactly nor her office, but a place to use for something other than sitting while waiting for traffic to move. No one walked in Denver and the city itself was spread over a hundred miles with a low profile except for the skyscrapers of 17th Street. Local civic cheerleaders often talked about it being "world class" and raved about new restaurants and the revitalized warehouse district downtown, but Sylvia wasn't impressed, especially since she never saw anything except from the car.

Frustrated with the city's lack of sophistication in the beginning, in time she'd gotten over wishing Denver were different and
accepted the city for what it was. But having grown up in what she
thought of as real cities where the main mode of transportation
was the bus or subway, she'd never completely adapted to Denver's
sprawling grid, the sea of cars stretching in every direction, the
sense that it was always rush hour. More striking than this was
the fact that traffic congestion appeared to bother no one else.
Stuck behind a semi belching smoke, she noticed a thin man in
a Mercedes tapping the steering wheel of his car in time to an
unheard tune while the woman next to her applied makeup and
talked in a cell phone.

She and Mitchell divided tasks with regard to the children and
since she seldom spent much time with Simon, today Sylvia was
taking him to Hebrew lessons. On the way, they would stop at a
donut shop. Because her son was so intensely in the moment, she
had worked out a game based on anticipation. "What kind of a
doughnut are you going to get today?" Sylvia asked now.

"Cherry filled," Simon said quickly. He was gazing out the window at the car lots going by on Colorado Boulevard.

"What if they're out of cherry filled?"

"Then I'll get a chocolate éclair."

"And if they're all out of those?"

The boy looked at her out of the corner of his eye, suspicious
that he was being worked in some way, which of course he was. "How
about those cake doughnuts they have, the ones with jimmies?"

"Good choice, one of my favorites. But what if they're even out
of those?"

"It's a doughnut shop, right?" Simon said. "Are they out of everything? I mean, do they have any doughnuts at all?"

"I don't know," Sylvia said. "Maybe they have them all. We're
just playing a game because we're stuck in traffic. But it's good to
plan ahead."

"Be prepared," Simon said, "like the Boy Scouts. Okay," he smiled, getting into it now. "If they're out of cake doughnuts, I'd get a chocolate raised, and if they're out of those, I'll get a honey-dipped, and if they're out of those I'd go for a chocolate or maple long john, and if they're even out of those, I'll get an old-fashioned." He paused dramatically. "They're never out of old fashioned doughnuts. Any questions?"

Sylvia laughed. "You're too good. I think you've got the doughnut question settled." She hadn't known there were that many kinds of doughnuts in the world. Clearly her son paid closer attention to what was going on around him than she had imagined.

Simon rocked back and forth in his seat laughing uproariously and his joy in having won caused a shiver in Sylvia's back and nearly brought tears to her eyes. Not for the first time she wondered how she could love this boy so much more than she did his father. And not for the first time, she felt vaguely guilty at this recognition.

Sylvia did not believe in falsely encouraging her patients. She knew that depression often hastened further decline but when she saw Thomas Morris for a follow-up appointment she became concerned. He no longer bantered with her and seemed disinclined to talk about his career or even about music in a general way. The malar rash had faded, but his joints were increasingly affected now and she worried about a persistent cough that could signal the lung problems that often came along with lupus. Usually, patients with a chronic illness died of some unrelated illness, like pneumonia, because of their lack of physical activity which was why doctors often got them up and moving, even in the hospital immediately after surgery. Thomas, however, showed no interest when she suggested physical therapy.

"I think I'll take a nap instead," he said. "If that's all right with you."

After he left, Sylvia scanned her bookshelves for a journal she had been reading that described a new protocol being developed in New Haven for patients with lupus. The results were preliminary because the protocol was so new, but the article interested her because the treatment seemed to have helped some patients whose disease was more advanced than Thomas'. After re-reading the journal, Sylvia contacted the author, who agreed that Thomas would be a likely candidate. The doctor was interested to learn that he was a musician and agreed to make the necessary arrangements with the hospital. But when Sylvia called his insurance company, the gatekeeper who answered her call seemed bored by her questions. And when Sylvia persisted, she was passed on to the physician reviewer who, to Sylvia's surprise, was familiar with the protocol.

"We consider this an experimental procedure," the reviewer said.

"Of course it's experimental," Sylvia said. "Everything we try for lupus patients is experimental. If there were a cure, there'd be no need for further research."

The reviewer wasn't convinced. "We're not in the business of funding research, Doctor," she said. "We're providing health care. It's different."

"I know that," Sylvia said and took a deep breath. Fighting wouldn't help Thomas. "You can't do research without patients," she said. "That's obvious. And you can't provide good care without taking chances in treatment. This patient is getting worse despite all we're doing, so clearly it's not enough. You're his insurance company so you're responsible for his care, and so am I."

"I'm sorry he's so sick," the reviewer said, and she sounded genuinely sympathetic. Sylvia had a moment of empathy for the doctor on the other end of the line. No one wanted to work for insurance companies turning down claims but at least she was talking to another doctor. It could have been worse. "Mr. Morris isn't the only person we insure or the only patient you treat, Doctor," the reviewer said now. "Do you have any idea how many low-birth-weight babies could be treated for the money it would cost to send him to New Haven for a month? Or how many physicals or well-baby examinations? Do you think we should provide heroic treatment for a few people who might never get well or do the best we can for the largest number of people?"

"I know that, Jesus," Sylvia muttered. It was the standard managed care speech. It even made economic sense, but it was in direct conflict with the Hippocratic oath and her personal beliefs. "Look," Sylvia said. "You're a doctor so you know the reason American medical care is the best in the world is because of specialists, because of experimental treatments, because someone somewhere gave a damn and took a chance."

She hoped appealing to the reviewer as a colleague would help, but she seemed imperturbable. "That's true," the reviewer said. "As far as it goes."

"Well, exactly how far is that?" Sylvia asked. "Does taking better care of everyone mean that we can't do our best for the individual patient? I'm not asking for a heart by-pass for an eighty-year old man or plastic surgery for a terminal cancer patient. Thomas Morris is a relatively young man with his life before him. If this protocol helped, it's possible that he could return to a full, productive career."

"If it did, it would," the reviewer said. "But, as you said yourself, there is no guarantee of that. We just can't approve things that haven't been demonstrated to be effective clinically. Success with a small number of patients over a limited period of time isn't the same thing. If we approved claims like that, it would raise premiums for everyone else."

"And cut into corporate profits." Sylvia thought of the lavish annual banquet the company always held, and the color-coordinated executive offices.

"Well, we are a business," the reviewer said briskly. "No one ever suggested otherwise. Is there anything else, Doctor?"

"Not unless you can tell me what to tell my patient."

"Don't tell him anything. This is a privileged conversation. There is no record of it. Officially, it never took place."

"You mean I can't even let Mr. Morris know this treatment exists?"

"Not while you're on our panel. Read your contract. We have the right to restrict information to all patients. We don't believe in raising false hopes."

Sylvia knew about gag rules. Though some states had moved to make them illegal, individual doctors had been removed from insurance panels and lost their practices for telling patients about treatments not approved by their insurance companies. It wasn't as if the doctor who designed the new protocol was some faith healer. He was a professor at Yale and she had read about his research in the New England Journal of Medicine. Sylvia thought again of Hippocrates. First, do no harm, the oath went, which was relatively easy. No one set out to purposely harm her patients. But what about sins of omission? Had she compromised herself ethically without even knowing it when she signed her contract?

"I don't think you have to worry about hope at all," Sylvia said now. "But you're saying that if I even mention to Mr. Morris that this treatment exists, you'll exclude me from the panel?"

"I can't speak for management," the reviewer. "But it could happen. You have a nice day now, Doctor."

The whole thing was Orwellian. Sylvia was supposed to pretend experimental procedures weren't available because the insurance company wouldn't pay for them. Sylvia was in no position to say for certain whether the new protocol would help Thomas Morris or anyone else. But he had a right to know everything about his condition. To pretend otherwise was not only unethical but insane.

She picked up her phone and began to dial before setting it down again. The fact that this new treatment had helped a few patients with lupus said little about whether it would help Thomas. She was irritated with the insurance company but could she justify sending him and his wife on a long, expensive trip that might very well fail to stop the progress of his disease?

She wondered if her affection for Thomas had her grasping at straws. Would she be reading medical journals into the night and going to the mat with the insurance company for a patient who was less accomplished, less charming, or less convinced of her brilliance? She settled the phone in its cradle and decided to think more about all of this before taking action one way or another.

When Sylvia was troubled by a case, she often consulted a neurologist named Luther Miller, who had been one of her teachers in medical school and still had an office at the university. Luther was tall and slightly stooped and lived in an old mansion in what he called the "two block historic district" of Denver. When she called, he suggested that she come by his house for coffee after work in the afternoon. They met in an elegant parlor with a gas fireplace and velvet club chairs. It was what she imagined the consulting rooms of doctors had been like a century ago, before managed care.

After she described the situation with Thomas Morris, Luther sat silently for a studying her, his long, intelligent face a little sad, or perhaps it was only the light. "How are things with you and Mitchell?" he asked suddenly.

This caught Sylvia off balance, though she had always discussed her life openly with Luther. "The same, I guess. He's become interested in philately."

Luther looked amused by this. "Stamp collecting? I don't think I know anyone who does that."

"Mitchell does. Recently he found a 4 cent Lincoln with a reversed face which excited him. Mitchell has interests that are unique. That's his talent."

"And we all need one, don't we?" Luther hesitated and drank some coffee. "I asked because I remember when you were a medical student you had a tendency to become over-involved with some patients."

Sylvia blushed. "This isn't the same thing," she said, "I haven't been a medical student for a long time." But Luther had touched a nerve. "It's different," she said quietly.

"I don't doubt you," Luther said. "But when you say things between you and Mitch are the same you're also saying nothing has resolved or improved. I understand you're not in love with this patient, but you wouldn't be the first doctor who became overly interested in a brilliant patient and in the process became a bit less objective in making judgments. Isn't that possible, Sylvia?"

Sylvia nodded. Luther was right, which was why she had come to see him. She wanted to examine her clinical judgment. "I see that," she said. "But I really don't believe I'm letting the situation with Mitchell influence me in this case." Sylvia realized that she sounded defensive. The way she dealt with her marriage was by purposely not thinking about it, not by transferring emotions that would logically have belonged there to her patients. Her ability to separate one from the other had worked reasonably well so far but Luther was right to raise the question.

Luther nodded. "I only mention it because I'm very fond of you and care about what happens in your life. You're a very talented young physician and you care deeply about your patients, but over-involvement is something to think about before inviting trouble with the insurance company. I'm not defending them, god knows. I've never had anything to do with insurance or case managers. Fortunately, my practice came to an end just as managed care was beginning to take hold here. I'm grateful for that."

"Thanks for saying I'm young," Sylvia said. "I mentioned that a patient said I looked older and Mitchell agreed with her."

Luther smiled. "Don't be ridiculous," he said. "Of course I have you by forty years give or take."

Have you read about this protocol?" Sylvia asked, trying to get back to her reason for coming.

"I have," Luther said. "And I think it's promising, but I'd feel better if they had a few thousand more patients and ten years of results."

Sylvia nodded. "Of course it would be more prudent to wait before trying anything experimental, but Thomas may be dead before that happens."

Luther sighed. "An interesting man. I've heard him play and it would be a loss. But that's always the problem, isn't it? At least with experimental procedures."

"What would you do in my case?" Sylvia asked. "Would you go to the patient with this unproven technique or keep quiet like the insurance company says?"

"I'd probably tell him just out of spite, because they said not to, but I'm not recommending that," Luther said quickly. "The more important question is the one you raised before, the ethical concern of encouraging false hopes. What chance is there that this could really help? And if it couldn't should you tell him anyway, figure that hope is his problem, not yours?"

"Is that fair to them?"

Luther smiled. "That's why I asked if you're over-involved. You're worried about being fair to this man, but adults make decisions based on the information in front of them. That doesn't need to be your concern."

"But people who are sick are in no position to make important decisions, especially about unfamiliar disciplines," Sylvia objected. "They're in a panic; desperate for anything that might conceivably work. Health articles in newspapers, magazines, and programs on television or things they read on the internet all seem relevant. There's too much information out there and most of it is useless."

"Sometimes less than useless," Luther said. "I agree." He stopped and looked into the fire. Then he continued. "This is what makes what we do difficult—and important. As your patient's doctor, your responsibility is to recognize the desperation, but realize that ultimately you can't protect anyone from himself. All you can do is provide the information; they'll have to make their own choices."

"Thomas Morris is a brilliant man," Sylvia said. "But how could he or any patient understand all the nuances of a disease like lupus? He hasn't studied it for years like we have."

Luther laughed quietly. "No one ever plans to get sick," he said. "That's what makes it so hard. If only we knew what we'd get, we could plan ahead intelligently. As it is, we're always playing catch-up, even if we're physicians. But everyone has to die of something, Sylvia."

"Given the possibilities lupus isn't a good way to go," Sylvia said.

Luther nodded sadly. Then they drank coffee in front of the fire and talked about other things for another hour after which Sylvia rose to go. "What have you decided?" Luther asked when he walked her to the door.

"I'm going to look for another job," she said.

Back in her office, Sylvia went back over Thomas' file. She rechecked the blood work, her notes from the physical exam. One thing that had drawn her to neurology was the elegance of the diagnostic techniques, the reliance on the physician's observations rather than tests alone, the importance of judgment and comparisons with other patients. Luther had taught this well and she had never forgotten his lectures about the importance of listening. Perhaps that was why she became over-involved. But as he said: no one ever planned to get sick. It caught patients by surprise, fooled as they were by the lax habits of good health. They were bewildered, scared, often in despair.

Ironically, managed care had actually aided some doctors in this respect. Because of the requirements of insurance companies for extensive tests and lab work, a physician's analytical skills had become progressively less crucial in medical treatment. She could remain removed and rely on the data. The insurance companies were primarily concerned about liability and in this regard they were no different than doctors who saw their malpractice insurance costs going through the roof. But Sylvia didn't need more test results in this instance. She knew very well what she was looking at.

Nevertheless, she reviewed. Her diagnosis had been made through analysis of the ANA titre in Thomas' blood. The rest of the file consisted of her case notes. More significant was what wasn't there. Instead of the patient's prognosis, she had simply written, "guarded" in the chart, which might mean anything. But she knew Thomas was likely to suffer from vasculitis, clotting disorders or kidney disease after a while. He might have to be dialyzed or even contract restrictive lung disease.

Still, what would be the purpose in describing the probable progress of the disease in this instance? The whole thing was a mystery that they were probing together. The point was, finally, that maintaining hope was essential when facing a serious illness. Even false hope was better than nothing which settled it for her.

She snapped the file shut and put it back in the drawer next to her desk. She respected the process she had gone through, and knew it was important, but her decision was essentially the same. She felt she had no choice. For a moment she was overwhelmed with responsibility, with the kind of power she held over her patients and the trust they placed in her. It made her nauseous at times but she also knew it was precisely this that had impelled her to choose a clinical practice over research. It was the reason she had so little respect for her husband with his little three-by-five cards and stamp books. She shook her head to rid herself of the image. Mitchell had nothing to do with this; she couldn't think about him now. She often told herself at three AM that she shouldn't be so obsessive, should put things away she couldn't resolve or affect, accept the inevitable. Which was true, but if she had been that kind of person she probably wouldn't be doing what she was doing. She would have stayed in philosophy and perhaps even become more like Mitchell.

She sighed in the empty office. Then she picked up the telephone and dialed. When Thomas Morris answered, she said, "Thomas, I'd like you and Betsy to come down and see me. We need to talk. There's a new treatment for lupus they're working on at Yale and I think you should know about it."

CHAPTER FOUR

Sylvia sat in the restaurant channeling *Anna Karenina.* If it is true, she thought, that families can be either a source of joy or heartbreak, it's equally true that in-laws are seldom either, though they might sometimes rise to the level of disappointment. Except in her case. What made more sense than her marriage to Mitchell was Sylvia's relationship with her father-in-law, a pathologist who from the start took an unusual interest in her and encouraged her in ways her own father never had. It was Gregory who first raised the possibility of Sylvia's going into medicine when she tired of graduate school and advanced her the money for medical school. This was generous of Gregory, but it had greater meaning for Sylvia because she'd never received any encouragement for future study from her own father, an accountant who didn't believe women should work outside the home.

But as much as she loved and admired Gregory, Sylvia wasn't married to him and their relationship wasn't enough to hold her marriage together. She and Mitchell had separated once when Sylvia had a brief infatuation with another intern only to be talked back together again by their parents who felt divorce would be a blot on the family name. Then Simon was born followed quickly by Becky and a separation seemed impossible for what it would mean for the children.

In the midst of these thoughts, however, Sylvia doubled back on herself as she did whenever she considered her disappointment in her husband. Was she so perfect? The answer was obvious, but perfect or not something needed to change. She hated the rhythm their marriage had taken on with her nagging, pushing, wanting Mitchell to magically transform into a man she could admire and love. When, predictably, he resisted this, she resented him even more and withdrew. It was unfair, perhaps more than unfair, but it was the way things were.

Even more troubling than all this, however, was the feeling that life was passing her by. Most of Sylvia's colleagues would say she had achieved a great deal, but she continued to be dogged by the suspicion that she was out of place, falling behind, among the gray hordes of ordinary doctors who had showed early promise then settled into their practices. She knew there was nothing wrong with this, yet she continued to note the ages of successful women in magazine articles and read her alumni magazine glumly registering the successes of her classmates. She had won no grants, published few articles, and conducted no groundbreaking research. Yet when she tried to express her dissatisfaction to those who might reasonably understand, her parents, her husband, they seemed perplexed by the question. She made a good living and was well thought of in the community so what was the problem? Her mother said she was just tired and offered to take her to a spa.

She didn't know if Mitchell might have talked to his parents about the tension in their marriage. He wasn't open with them but he might well have said something, if not to his father then to his mother, with whom he was closer. Sylvia treasured her relationship with Gregory, but it would be unreasonable to expect

Mitchell's parents not to side with their son. If Mitchell had said anything, Gregory would be too discreet to mention it, but in time she'd know. If they were to divorce, Sylvia wouldn't miss her mother-in-law, but in many ways Gregory made up for things lacking in her own family. Martha had inherited money from the family business and as a result Gregory was able to make a comfortable life in academic medicine without having to worry about finances. They drove used cars, but lived well and traveled when they wanted to. When Sylvia had needed money for medical school it was Gregory, not her own father, who had been there to help. She protested at the time that this was too much to ask, but Gregory just smiled and quoted Trollope: "'Money is worth thinking about,'" he said. "'But it's not worth thinking about very much'" Besides, you're not asking; I'm offering. There's a difference. You'll pay it back when you can."

Which was true. In addition to making her way through school in the shortest possible amount of time, Sylvia had borne two children and won the most prestigious prizes at graduation. "Best investment I ever made," Gregory said proudly at the ceremony.

Now as she watched Gregory moving slowly through the tables to meet her, she felt a sudden pang of expectant loss. Sylvia watched him with affection as he approached, a dapper little man, his silver hair neatly barbered, wearing a tweed jacket and a crimson foulard tie. Like his son, he was careful about his appearance, even a bit vain, but it didn't bother her. What was stranger was how completely different he was from Mitchell in other way, his passion about his research, his enjoyment in her accomplishments.

She rose to meet Gregory and leaned into him, feeling his cheek paper thin against her lips, aware as she always was what a small, delicate man he was, feeling like a behemoth as her arms encircled his body and they embraced. "Happy Birthday," she said. "How are you?"

Gregory sat down and drank from his water glass. Sylvia noticed his hands shaking slightly, a pre-Parkinsonian tremor, she guessed, but she didn't let her neurologist's mind go there. "I could complain," he said, "but who would listen? I wouldn't even listen myself."

"I'd listen," Sylvia said.

Gregory smiled thinly and patted her hand. "You need to learn not to take everything so seriously, honey. It's what I like about you, that urgency, the attention to every problem in the world. But I'll tell you it's going to take you away before your time. You've got to lighten up, at least some of the time. Anyway, what's more boring than listening to old people complain about their health?"

It seemed odd to hear Gregory using the vernacular but he wasn't the first person to tell her to relax. "You're not old," she said.

Gregory smiled again, his teeth small and white in thin lips. "Seventy-eight is old," he said sharply. He didn't want to be patronized but Sylvia was actually protecting herself. As long as he wasn't old he would never die and she wouldn't have to live without him.

"Okay, then. You don't seem old to me," she corrected herself. "Are you still playing tennis?"

Gregory shrugged. "If you call four old codgers trying desperately not to race after balls they can't reach playing tennis, I suppose I am," he said. "Hey, let's order."

They ate salmon and salad and drank white wine. Gregory asked about the children and briefly described his current research grant. Then he said, "How's your husband anyway?"

This was a loaded question but Sylvia knew Gregory didn't want a direct answer. He had been neither a good husband nor a good father, but he still seemed to value the institution of marriage. He'd proved that when he joined with her parents and practically bribed her to return to Mitchell after they separated briefly two years into their marriage. "I wonder if Mitchell's mentioned Simon's bar mitzvah to you?" she asked. He was only twelve, but he was already taking lessons with a private tutor in Hebrew.

Neither Martha nor Gregory had ever belonged to a synagogue though Gregory had once mentioned attending a Zionist day camp in Wisconsin in his youth. Now he looked mystified. "How old is Simon anyway? Well, that's stupid. If he's having a bar mitzvah he must be twelve or thirteen."

"Next June," Sylvia said gently.

Gregory nodded and took a breadstick. "I've never gone in for any of that," he said. "As you know."

"But it's important to me," Sylvia said, "so I hope you'll come anyway. It's a ritual, like a bris. That has meaning, doesn't it?"

Gregory shifted in his chair. As close as they had been, intimacy had always made him uncomfortable. "Of course," he said. "How but in ceremony are innocence and beauty born?"

Sylvia smiled at the old man showing off. Gregory had often said he was appalled at the lack of culture in the young doctors he trained and he liked to remind them that Smollett, Chekhov and William Carlos Williams had all been physicians. "Of course, Yeats was writing about a girl," Sylvia said, teasing him.

"His daughter, I know. Doesn't matter," Gregory said. "But that's very good, Sylvie. Damned few doctors your age spend time reading Irish poetry."

"Or American, for that matter. Didn't Emerson say the poet was the true physician of the soul?"

"Now you're showing me up and you're not even sweating," Gregory said. "Anyway, just let Martha know when the bar mitzvah is and we'll be there and buy the lunch."

Sylvia hadn't meant to ask for anything, but she was touched as always by Gregory's generosity. She put her hand on his. "I appreciate that. I just thought Mitchell might have mentioned it."

"Why in god's name would Mitch say anything about that?" Gregory asked. "He almost never comes by or talks to us as it is. He's probably less Jewish than I am, and that's saying something."

Sylvia laughed, which pleased Gregory. She had never known anyone who combined erudition and common sense in such a fluid way. Mainly, though, she liked talking, just being with him. It was love. "So he hasn't mentioned anything about the ceremony, about aliyahs, anything?"

Gregory wasn't smiling anymore. "Instead of asking the same question over and over, why don't you just say whatever it is you want to say, honey? We've known each other for too long to beat around the bush this way."

But Sylvia found she couldn't, not yet, and she thought Gregory suspected anyway. "I know it seems trivial to you," she said lamely. "I just don't want to ruin things for Simon."

"Or for you?" Gregory said.

"For everyone," Sylvia said.

Gregory was silent. "I don't think there's really much any of us have to say or do about it as long as we behave. Mitch's going to be involved as much as he wants to be, I guess, so that leaves the organizing up to you. Not surprising, but Mitch isn't an emotional person. I don't know anything about what he's thinking. I never have and I've known him all his life."

Gregory laid his napkin on the table in a gesture of finality and Sylvia was sorry she'd brought the subject up. She supposed she wanted Gregory to understand how difficult her position was but in the end he was Mitchell's father and that trumped their friendship, whatever illusions she might have previously allowed herself. Now a kind of cool civility had replaced the warm good humor of a few minutes before.

"I'm sorry," she said. "I shouldn't have said anything."

"No harm done," Gregory said briskly. "And congratulations to Simon. Let me know what he wants in the way of a gift. Got to go."

Then he was gone with the briefest of hugs and Sylvia was left alone, wondering if in the future she might remember the unplanned consequence of this lunch to be a severing of ties to

Gregory. No matter what happened with Mitchell she wouldn't want that, but she knew that often enough ineluctable things occur that are not the result of anyone's planning.

In the rush of office visits and family responsibilities Sylvia hadn't thought much about Thomas Morris before their next appointment, but when he came in for his office visit he seemed out of sorts. She asked what was the matter.

"Nothing, really, "he said. "Beyond the fact that I have this illness, which I mostly accept. I wish I didn't have to spend half my life in various doctors' offices. Not you," he said quickly. "But I'm always going to the hospital for tests I've already had and treatments I've never heard of that I doubt will do any good."

"Frustrating," Sylvia agreed. He had become part of the medical system, she thought. While he may have wanted to think of his doctor and all of the nurses and technicians as caregivers and himself as the recipient of all of their caring, the idea that such kindness must be organized, manipulated, or to use the medical term, titrated by an unseen authority in some other city annoyed him. "That's managed care," she said now. "We're all part of a team. Your team, if you want to think of it that way."

"Go, team," he said without enthusiasm. "But isn't it all sort of ridiculous? I mean how do you manage care exactly, always giving just the right amount, but not too much? Then there's the business of managing caring, I suppose? Maybe that's related?"

"Something like that," Sylvia said. She found the humor helpful. Then, "This really bothers you, doesn't it?" Sylvia had a habit of directness and it was more than simply being chronically in a hurry. She would have been the same way if they had the whole afternoon before them. In any case, she was virtually unable to hold anything back, or at least anything significant, as if whatever she held inside would destroy her if she failed to let it go.

Her question seemed to unsettle him. He wasn't a convention-ally handsome man but she had the feeling he was accustomed to having the upper hand with women. "It does," he admitted slowly. "But I'm not sure why. I think I've always gotten whatever care I needed."

"So far, you mean?"

Thomas nodded. "I suppose that's it. The idea that it isn't up to me or even to you whether or not I can come in here if I feel the need. The implied suggestion that I might be a malingerer and therefore someone has to check first to make sure it's really neces-sary. That seems to be there in all these tests and scans. I mean, everyone knows my diagnosis. There's no mystery about it. Why would anyone want to come to the doctor's office if he weren't sick? No offense," he said quickly.

"None taken," Sylvia said. "But you'd be surprised at the num-ber of people who just come in to talk rather than for medical reasons."

"Like me," Thomas said. "Doesn't that make you feel a little futile? That all you can do for them is listen?"

If it did, Sylvia thought, she should have chosen a different ca-reer. Most of the diseases she dealt with had no cure or effective treatment, but that wasn't why she had chosen neurology. She had been drawn to it because of the fascination of what was difficult if not impossible to diagnose and treat. "Not really," Sylvia said. "I never thought of medicine as being an absolute or myself as some kind of miracle worker. I don't expect to cure everything or help everyone, and sometimes listening is the best treatment anyway. Still, I'm sorry you feel the way you do. I'm not crazy about this new system myself, but I suppose there were some abuses before."

She was wearing a white jacket with a burgundy skirt under-neath that was short enough to reveal her long, slender legs. She was aware of Thomas furtively examining them but she didn't want to embarrass him by covering up. She was used to men openly admiring her and as long as it didn't go any further than that she felt flattered rather than insulted. Now, as if reading her mind, Thomas looked away, and examined her diploma wall: University of Chicago for her B.S. and then California for medical school. Another certificate announced that she was certified by the national board of neurology. "I'm taking your time," he said apologetically.

She shrugged. "What am I here for? You're my patient; I'm your caregiver."

They laughed together and the room seemed larger. "What sort of abuses?" Thomas asked.

Sylvia looked at the ceiling and let out her breath. "I get a call from the Emergency Department," she said. "A patient's walked in off the street complaining that he fainted, but they can't find anything wrong with him. WADAO."

Thomas raised his eyebrows.

Sylvia smiled. "Medical slang. It's an acronym for 'weak and dizzy all over', but it covers a lot of territory."

"That's me," Thomas said. "But these people you're talking about, there was nothing wrong?"

"They had symptoms," Sylvia said. "So you didn't know if there was anything wrong or not and you always have to make sure. So I'd go down to the hospital and examine them, but most of the time there'd be nothing to treat. Like I said about my patients before. It's not unusual."

"They didn't need any care?"

"Not really. At least not in a professional way I could provide."

"So that's abuse? Of what? Who was hurt?"

"Maybe abuse is the wrong word but it's not what our medical facilities are here for. Hospitals are incredibly expensive to maintain and so is a doctor's time. You don't want to call on them unless it's really necessary. This new system weeds out those people that don't really need to be treated, at least those who are insured.

They can't go in without permission from their primary doctor and the doctors down there can't just send them on to me without a referral. All in all it lets specialists be more effective doctors, make better use of our time."

Thomas' expression was quizzical. But they're still WADAO?" he said. "The patients, I mean."

Sylvia nodded. "I don't mean to sound glib," she said. She hated to feel like an apologist or lackey of the insurance companies who were funding the whole system and paying her salary. Not for the first time she wondered how she had gotten to this place in life, what if anything it had to do with the way she had conceived of a medical practice as a younger woman. She had imagined working on an Indian reservation or maybe in some under-served community in Appalachia. She'd read about Doctors Without Borders and thought about taking her residency in Africa or Brazil. But none of that had happened. She'd married Mitchell and here they were. There was no room for idealism in the current scheme of things.

Sylvia leaned forward on her elbows. It seemed important that she explain her position in more detail to Thomas. "The flaw in the system is that a small minority of those people who wander into the ED and are confused will have brain tumors or neurological diseases that might go untreated because no one is following them, but to the insurance companies the key word is small. Medicine isn't being practiced for the extraordinary patient anymore, the unusual case, and everyone is being encouraged to treat themselves if they can. We pass out helpful informational packets. You probably saw them out in the receptionist's office. Anyway, most of the people we miss won't sue anyone." She smiled wryly then shook herself, as if the thought had given her a chill. "But this has nothing to do with you," she said briskly. "As you said, you have a diagnosis and your treatment plan has been approved."

"But I still can't come in whenever I want," Thomas said. "I have to call Dr. Simpson and he has to okay it." This seemed to be a sticking point to Thomas. It was as if he expected physicians to be on call, to work only for him and satisfy his every need. She suspected this went beyond his illness and had something to do with having been pampered in his life as a concert artist. Still she didn't blame him for not liking his primary care doctor, the gatekeeper in the current parlance. The insurance companies made it worth Simpson's while to avoid referring all but the most serious cases to specialists by allotting him only a certain amount of money each year for that purpose, irrespective of how many patients he might see. In the managed care business this was referred to as capitation, but Sylvia thought of it as decapitation because it interfered with her ability to practice medicine as she thought she should.

"Have you had trouble with Dr. Simpson's office?"

Thomas shifted in his chair. Sylvia knew he didn't like Simpson much and though she would never have said so, Sylvia shared his feelings. "Not exactly," Thomas said.

Sylvia spread her hands before her. "Inexactly, then? Well, you let me know if you do." She wrote something on one of her cards. "This is my direct number; you don't have to go through the switchboard if it bothers you." Then she stood to end the interview.

CHAPTER FIVE

It was a clear August morning, sunny as usual but cool as Sylvia drove through town on her way to work. The kids were in summer camp at the Jewish Community Center, the swimming pool was open and for once everything seemed to be going according to schedule. Which did nothing to assuage the feeling of foreboding that was Sylvia's constant companion these days, the idea that an explosion was inevitable and that it might be hers.

She picked up coffee, walked through the reception area and went into her office. She'd been going to yoga classes lately and was trying to remember to do the breathing exercises they taught. Breathe and relax, relax and breathe, she told herself, but somehow it seemed to work less well for her than for the lissome instructors. Of course, she told herself. They're blonde and twenty, what problems can they have? She wondered if caffeine interfered with achieving perfect serenity then did the breathing exercises anyway. Afterwards, she sat at her desk looking over the list of patients she'd see today.

Sylvia's *satori* was short-lived as the first chart she examined annoyed her. This wouldn't bother her, she told herself, if it didn't happen every day. Her most important asset in treating a new patient was a complete medical history but what lay before her on the desk was virtually useless. She knew the primary care physician who had referred the patient only slightly but his scribbled note alluding to "Poss. syncope or ataxia," could mean almost anything or nothing at all.

She understood the demands under which the referring doctor worked and the necessity to get this chart off his desk and into someone else's hands. He, like everyone else, was chronically short of time. Time to listen, time to care who the patient was. Time to find out what really might be the trouble. Like her, he no doubt seldom knew his patients personally anymore. Small wonder patients were increasingly litigious and doctors had to spend time doing unnecessary tests to cover themselves. Nobody really found this rewarding, but it was their shared reality and Sylvia expected it to get worse.

Medicine was often described as being an art rather than a science, but it was never so true as in neurology. Diagnosis required patience, judgment, subtlety, and time. When she was younger Sylvia had imagined a future in which life would take on a manageable rhythm at some point. She supposed this could still happen. She was only 35 and had been in practice less than ten years but somehow it seemed less likely than before.

Sitting in her white lab coat with a patient's medical history spread out before her on the desk, however, she felt cool, unemotional, in charge, because it was always someone else's world she was managing. Even that was often a necessary illusion since disease presented itself without warning and then proceeded on its own schedule. She could observe and describe the condition and sometimes offer treatment but that was all.

Sylvia knew the calm she experienced as a doctor working with patients was crucial but it served the dual purpose of holding her personal world at bay. At times she'd rebel against the necessity of this, thinking she'd done nothing wrong except choose a husband for reasons of convenience rather than love. But what came back to her repeatedly late at night, was the idea that this was her last chance, even if she didn't know what *this* was exactly.

There was no answer. She only knew she felt a need to move, to do something differently. Now she stood and looked in her office mirror. She was tall and thin with thick black hair that looked a bit tangled in an attractive way. She knew she dressed well and anyone would say she was good looking, even pretty. Why shouldn't she have a chance at whatever might come that could improve her life in the future? Better yet, why did she hesitate to take that chance?

Of course, the middle-aged woman whose chart was in front of her wouldn't care nor should she. Still, Sylvia was surprised she had gotten the referral. Dizziness was something family practice doctors often thought they could handle themselves. Why should they take money from their own pockets to send patients Sylvia's way? This cut down on referrals to specialists, which to the insurance companies meant the system was working. It was good finance but not always good medicine.

Without a decent history, Sylvia would have to start from the beginning, something that would annoy her patient who would likely already have told the same story to several doctors. But it couldn't be helped. The differential diagnosis for dizziness, the list of things that could be causing it, was vast. Even the term was only an abstraction, meaning different things to different people. Sylvia took a deep breath, smoothed an errant eyebrow with her finger and went next door.

The examining room was small and painted a light blue that mimicked the patient's complexion. Mrs. Simmons was thin, with a narrow face and beady gray eyes, but her curly brown hair made her seem somehow soft. Her husband sat next to her on a stool too small for his bulk. Both had pinched expressions and the room smelled vaguely of sweat and after-shave. Sylvia understood. No one looked forward to coming to a specialist no matter what the symptoms were; everyone's first thought was cancer. She smiled in what she hoped was a reassuring way, and extended her hand. "Mrs. Simmons, I'm Dr. Rose. It's nice to meet you." She nodded at the husband. Mrs. Simmons swallowed air but said nothing, as if she were unable to speak.

Sylvia was used to patients being nervous; neurology was a daunting specialty known to the general public, if it was known at all, for the celebrity dinners held to raise money for incurable diseases with unpronounceable names. Now she sat in a chair and fixed her gaze on her patient, blocking out all other thoughts. "Mrs. Simmons, Dr. Peters sent you to see me because you've been experiencing some symptoms, but I want you to understand that just being here doesn't constitute a diagnosis. Right now, we just have some symptoms."

"You mean she ain't sick?" the husband asked hopefully.

Sylvia turned to the man and smiled again. "I don't know if she's sick or not, Mr. Simmons. I just met your wife. That's what we're here to find out. I want to take a history and examine her. But that's just a start."

"She ain't the same," the man said. "I'll tell you that right now. Not how she always was. She fell down the other morning and practically dropped a frying pan on the baby's head. That ain't normal."

Sylvia nodded. "You're right. That's not normal. What I meant was that sometimes people have transient episodes that come and go, and have no cause, at least none we can find. And sometimes those episodes don't recur. They happen once and then never happen again. We call those attacks idiopathic."

The word impressed the Simmons's, which gave Sylvia a chance to turn her attention back to the woman. The husband wasn't her patient and regardless of his relationship with his wife, he couldn't really tell Sylvia how she felt. "Mrs. Simmons, Dr. Peters said you've been having problems with dizziness at home. Could you tell me more about that?"

Mrs. Simmons looked perplexed by Sylvia's question, but it was important. Sylvia needed to understand what dizzy meant to Mrs. Simmons. Patients used dizziness to describe a variety of sensations, including light-headedness, faintness, a spinning sensation, mental confusion, headaches, blurred vision, and tingling in the arms or legs, all of which might indicate various diseases, anxiety, eyestrain, or nothing. In fact, in Sylvia's experience it was usually nothing identifiable. Simply saying, "Doctor, I'm dizzy," was almost meaningless but Sylvia had to start somewhere.

Mrs. Simmons' face screwed up in concentration. "It's like, all of a sudden my feet ain't there," she said.

Gait disturbances, Sylvia thought, and remembered Peters' note about ataxia. The differential on that ran a half-page in *Harrison's.* "Do you mean you can't feel your feet? That they're numb? Or do you have difficulty walking, maintaining your balance, when you go outside?"

The questions were frustrating for the woman because in her terror, Mrs. Simmons hadn't been able to consider her condition analytically or describe it very well. Now, suddenly, subtlety and precision were expected of her. Sylvia understood but she persisted and finally the woman said, "No, it wasn't like that. If I was out someplace, I could walk wherever I needed to go. It was more like my brain locked up and then my feet weren't there. Does that make sense?"

Sylvia sidestepped the question. None of it made sense without a larger context. "You mean you didn't feel your feet? Or just that they weren't working properly?" The woman seemed unable to answer this. Sylvia waited a moment, and then she asked, "Did you feel faint, Mrs. Simmons, or black out for any period of time when you couldn't feel your feet?"

Sylvia noticed that now her questions were having a calming effect, as if for Mrs. Simmons the process of trying to isolate and explain her condition was a relief from worrying about it. She was regaining color and her expression seemed less anxious. "No, I wasn't out cold or nothing, just not that steady, you know?"

Sylvia nodded. "Did it affect your vision in any way?"

Mrs. Simmons looked querulous. "I can see fine. Always could. The doctor said I've got great eyes." This was clearly a point of pride.

Sylvia tried to refine the question. "Was there any cloudiness, spots in front of your eyes or a black bar in the middle of your field of vision?"

Mrs. Simmons seemed to consider these possibilities interesting, ticking each one off on her fingers as Sylvia spoke. Then she looked at her husband and shrugged. "No, I didn't have none of that."

"Okay," Sylvia said. "Good." That ruled out syncope for the most part. She looked at the husband now. "Mr. Simmons, could you get up for a moment and let your wife sit on that stool?"

The man looked suspicious. "I'm staying in here," he said truculently.

Sylvia smiled. The husband was important. She needed him on her side. "Of course," she said. "I didn't mean that you should leave the room. I'd just like you to let your wife sit on the stool for a while, please." The man hesitated but finally got up to let his wife take his place on the stool

When the patient was seated, Sylvia took Mrs. Simmons by the shoulders and quickly spun her around. "Hey, what's going on?" Mr. Simmons said.

Sylvia ignored him. She stopped the woman and commanded, "Now, stand up."

When the woman did, she staggered into her husband who had to strain to hold her erect. After Mrs. Simmons had steadied herself, Sylvia asked, "Was that the kind of dizziness you were talking about?"

It was a standard clinical maneuver, an attempt to replicate what the patient was feeling and it had the desired effect. Mrs. Simmons looked addled but she smiled hesitantly as if she was pleased with her performance. "Yes, it was sort of like that," she said thoughtfully, looking at the stool as if it had caused all this.

Sylvia nodded again. Vestibular dysfunction could mean a great many things, but at least they were narrowing things down. Which was the point of the differential. It allowed her to rule out illnesses and focus on the actual complaint.

But Mr. Simmons had had enough. "So what does she have?" he asked abruptly. "What the hell is it?"

The man acted as if Sylvia were holding out on them, though her motives for doing so would be mysterious. She liked to be responsive, transparent but she had learned to be cautious about diagnosis. It wasn't normal to experience extreme dizziness but it would be a mistake to assume Mrs. Simmons' illness was something serious. As one of her professors in medical school had said, "If you hear hoofbeats, think horses, not zebras."

She smiled at Mr. Simmons, trying to project calm certainty and said, "I don't know if Mrs. Simmons has anything. You're asking me for a diagnosis before I know if your wife is really ill."

"Then can you please tell me what the hell we're doing here if you don't know nothing?" the husband asked.

It was a reasonable question. But it could take months to arrive at a diagnosis. In the meantime it was important to maintain an alliance not only with the patient but with her husband, no matter how impatient he might be. "We're here to find out if there's anything wrong with your wife, and if so, what it is," she said. "By talking to you and Mrs. Simmons today I've been able to rule out some things it might have been but isn't, and now I know what she means when she says she's been dizzy."

"That's something then, am I right?" Mr. Simmons said hopefully.

"Actually, it's a lot for the first examination," Sylvia said, "but this is going to go on for a while. I don't know when I'll know what's bothering your wife. I'll have to see Mrs. Simmons several times to find out more and we'll probably run some tests on her as well. You can make an appointment outside."

Back in her office, Sylvia put in a call to her husband, but Mitchell was still out. That morning he had told her he needed blocks of time to clear his head to schedule his out-of-town stops this week, after which he had another stamp meeting, this time in Memphis. Having little or not time for reflection herself, Sylvia resented Mitchell's projects, which always had to be undertaken in solitary splendor. Not that she really wanted to go to Memphis, but it was the principle of the thing that rankled her. A bare three weeks after the birth of their daughter Mitchell had flown off to England for some conference pleading the necessity of space. Sylvia wanted to scream that she was the one who needed space. She was in her last year of residency and had two small children to care for.

She knew that in a sense it was her own fault. She hadn't protested Mitchell's absence then. Instead, she smiled gamely and sent her husband off even as she wished he knew intuitively what she was feeling, knew that she needed him to be there, to take care of her and their home. Remembering that time, Sylvia realized it might have been the turning point in her marriage. Yet she'd done nothing.

She understood that in part her resentment was rooted in envy. She envied Mitchell not only his leisure but his relentless determination to indulge it. She was honest with herself about this but so far she'd expressed her frustration only through anger over petty things. She would blow up at Mitchell for his lack of financial acumen or incompetence in dealing with household projects.

It was odd since her father had certainly been as selfish, though in a different way. How, she wondered, could the two most important men in her life have this in common when it was the single thing that bothered her most? Why hadn't she known better? She couldn't say he'd changed. In fact, she had never known anyone who changed less than Mitchell or seemed more pleased with himself. It drove her crazy to think about it.

Still, there remained some affection between them and, miraculously, an occasional sexual flutter. Now, almost without thinking consciously about what she was doing, Sylvia began jotting down the differential diagnosis of a failed marriage on a prescription pad:

- Marriage was a mistake in the first place
- Few common interests or values
- Lack of love
- Shortage of money
- Little free time
- Divergent views of the future
- Children
- Frequent conflict

She stopped. Face it, she told herself. This diagnosis like those she dealt with in her work was many-faceted. In their case, all of the above were true, except conflict. They never fought or even raised their voices against one another. Probably they should have fought more. That could have helped them to stake out and refine their positions, but now it was too late. She couldn't change the dynamic of the relationship after a dozen years of marriage. She looked again at what she had written. Then she turned the tablet over and went back into the examining room to see her next patient.

Managed Care

Mrs. Simmons' dizziness did not disappear and the results of Sylvia's physical examination were inconclusive. The woman wasn't dizzy constantly and the spells hadn't worsened to the point that she was unable to live a normal life. Mrs. Simmons could go out by herself to shop and she certainly did not need someone with her at all times. There was, as far as tests could show, neither carcinoma nor pathologic vertigo. As Sylvia ruled things out and discussed the possibilities with the family, Mr. Simmons seemed to grow more cheerful, though his wife was still morose.

"That's another one down, Doc," he said when Sylvia met with the couple one dark Monday.

"Yes, Mr. Simmons. Your wife doesn't have cancer. We can say that for sure."

"And that's good, right?"

Sylvia agreed, though somewhat more cautiously than Mr. Simmons might have liked. It was always good not to have cancer, but since the symptoms had neither disappeared nor lessened, she was more convinced than before that something was seriously wrong. "I'm still concerned about your wife's condition," she said. "I had hoped this might resolve spontaneously."

"Maybe she's just tired," Mr. Simmons said sympathetically. "Those kids would give anyone a run for her money."

Sylvia nodded, but she felt sure now that this wasn't a transient condition. "I'd like to do some more tests," she said.

Mrs. Simmons started crying silently but her husband seemed to take Sylvia's comment as an insult. "You doctors ain't ever satisfied until you find something, are you? Even if there's nothing there, which is what you just said."

Sylvia couldn't let this pass. "That's not what I said, Mr. Simmons. I said Mrs. Simmons doesn't have cancer; she doesn't. But I do think there's something there, something abnormal. We just don't know what it is yet." There was no point in going further. Diseases of the central nervous system could often produce dizziness but were resistant to clear diagnosis. It took C-T scans, MRIs or lumbar punctures, painful and unpleasant procedures. And it took time.

Sometimes she thought of it as a problem of focus, like trying to pick out a single flower from a bouquet. She had to narrow her vision to the exclusion of everything else in order to know what she was really looking at. But Sylvia didn't explain this to Mr. Simmons because she doubted he'd respond to a simile. Illness might be fascinating to her, but it was unavoidably tragic and frustrating for patients and their families. Mrs. Simmons' dizziness was idiopathic--nothing seemed to have caused it directly--but it wasn't temporary. Eventually, the disease, whatever it was, would declare itself in some way, and when that happened, she would have to do what she could to treat it.

Meanwhile, it did her no good to have her patient's husband suspect her. Sylvia took Mrs. Simmons' hand and palpated the cold, rigid fingers gently. "It will be all right," she said. "We'll find out what's going on. Don't worry."

Mrs. Simmons' face was blue with white patches around her nose. Water stood in her eyes. "Do you really think so?"

"I do," Sylvia said and patted her patient's arm. "It will just take some more time." But in this instance she was afraid the passage of time would not bring reassurance.

Sylvia didn't know if Mitchell was happy and she seldom thought about it. She came from a family that valued money and property above all else, so she had sought out a man who had no interest in such matters, an intellectual disdainful of the pursuit of worldly things. Now ironically she found her husband wanting because he lacked the very things she'd married him for. She knew it was unfair but she couldn't help it. It wasn't as simple as wanting him to be more masculine or take on a more traditional male role, but that was certainly part of it. She may not have wanted to marry her father, a man who was an artist with a band saw and spent hours in his shop working on new projects for the house, but she hadn't wanted to marry her mother either.

Complicating all this in Sylvia's mind was what she considered to be the impossibility of confronting Mitchell with her concerns. He thought of himself as an aesthete and wanted nothing more than to live what he seriously called the life of the mind, odd as this sound for a representative of a suit company. This being so the opinions of others, who occupied a position lower on the depth chart in his mind, mattered little to him. There was a curious insularity to him, Sylvia thought but for Mitchell it worked

The phone interrupted these thoughts and she picked it up, her annoyance apparently showing in her voice. "Did I pick a bad time?" Thomas Morris said.

Sylvia shook her head. "No, this is fine. How can I help you, Thomas?"

"I don't know, are you sure it's all right. You said I could call you on your private line. After all, you're my caregiver, right?"

His attempt to regain the flirtatious jauntiness she had noticed in their first interview touched Sylvia. "Yes, I am," she said. "Is everything okay?"

"Relatively, you mean?"

"Yes, that's what I meant." No euphemisms for this man.

"I read somewhere that there's a way to get help with wheelchairs, parallel bars, things like that. Is that right?"

He was telling her indirectly that he needed such things, that his condition was deteriorating faster than they had hoped. She looked quickly at her PDA and saw that their last appointment had been only two weeks before. This wasn't a good sign. "Are you having trouble walking?"

"I'm having trouble with everything," he said. "You name it. Standing up, shaving, combing my hair, eating breakfast. In a way, walking is easier that other things since you're really just losing your balance over and over. I'm good at losing my balance."

Sylvia felt her eyes tear up. The man's determination to remain as he had been was moving but she didn't want to let on how she was feeling. She picked up her notepad. "Social workers normally handle those things," she said, "but there's no reason I can't do it for you."

"I could call them," Thomas said hesitantly.

"No," Sylvia said. "This is fine. I'll make the contact for you. If someone doesn't get back to you in a day or so, just call me again. And I'll see you as soon as you want."

"Looking forward to it," Thomas said, as if they were making a lunch date. Then he was gone.

Hanging up, Sylvia was impressed with Thomas' courage and she was flattered by his interest in her. She couldn't remember the last time Mitchell had noticed her legs. Of course her relationship with Thomas was unequal—she was his doctor; he was dependent on her. But the fact that a reasonably well-known concert artist would admire her more than her own husband made an impact on her. And even Mitchell's insensitivity to others would have been acceptable, had she felt he gave her something emotionally. She rationalized that he might simply have very little to give, that she couldn't blame him for being limited. But that didn't make it any easier to be married to the man.

On summer evenings, after the dinner dishes had been cleared and the children were in bed, Sylvia and Mitchell would sit on the back porch in the half-hour before bedtime, drinking tea and talking. The conversation had never been particularly stimulating, but previously Sylvia had enjoyed these evenings. It was comfortable in the darkness and seemed like a reward for the difficulty of the day. Mitchell wasn't exciting, but he was companionable. Tonight, they repeated the ritual, as if repetition itself could confer meaning. Yet it felt perfunctory, as if each of them was afraid to speak openly.

Actually, Sylvia thought it was worse than this: the truth was they had nothing to say to each other.

In the half-light, she studied her husband in profile. He was neither tall nor short. He had small, squinty eyes behind wire-rimmed glasses, and a nervous mouth. His high forehead was made ridiculous by a Maginot line of hair plugs he had inserted the year before. Mitchell was quite pleased with the treatment and took the opportunity to indulge in some silk Italian shirts which he wore open necked with a gold chain. While the plugs did give him the hair line he'd lacked, even a gentle breeze could disturb Mitchell's pompadour, leaving hair in his face and a pink scalp exposed. Sylvia had thought of suggesting that he shave it close to the scalp, but often the best strategy was simply to turn away. Not that age hadn't affected her, but Sylvia didn't need to be sexually attracted to herself. Tonight, for reasons she didn't know, she asked: "Are you happy?"

Mitchell didn't reply immediately but she knew he had heard because he started polishing his glasses furiously, a sure sign that he was thinking. Finally, he replied, "Happy? What do you mean? In what sense?"

It was hopeless. A simple question brought forth intellectual inquiry. Sylvia drained her cup and rose to her feet. "Forget it," she said. "I'm just tired."

"No," Mitchell said. "I'm interested. Tell me what you mean."

Sylvia didn't have the energy or desire for an abstruse discussion and was sorry now she had said anything. "Exactly what I said. Are you happy? It's not really a difficult question, is it? Not hard to grasp."

Mitchell smiled a lazy smile, as if this was a trick question and the answer was elusive but worth pursuing. He replaced his glasses and turned to face her, a small smile on his face. "Do I seem happy to you?"

"I don't know, Mitchell," Sylvia said. "I have no idea. That's why I asked." The fact was he didn't seem much of anything. Neither happy nor unhappy, neither excited nor lethargic, neither up nor down. He seemed nothing; a cipher, which was an awful thing to say or even think of her husband, and she knew it. And if Mitchell were unhappy, Sylvia blamed herself in part, even if she had no idea what his grievances might be.

"It's hard to know," Mitchell said, warming to his subject. "One must first define happiness, I suppose, before deciding if it's something that's available to one, if it's something achievable in life."

Which clinched it for Sylvia. An overwhelming weariness took possession over. She didn't know why she'd asked but she thought she was trying to have an honest, if indirect, conversation about their situation. "I'm going to bed," she said, leaving Mitchell looking disappointed that a conversation that had seemed so promising had inexplicably come to an abrupt end.

The Simmons' were again in Sylvia's office, though now a brother in a nylon cap advertising a trucking company had joined them. Time for some answers, Sylvia figured; she only wished she had more of them.

"The results of the CT-scan and Mrs. Simmons' MRI are back," she began, "so we need to talk about those."

Mr. Simmons took his wife's hand, steeling himself for the worst, though it wasn't clear what the worst would be in his mind. Before Sylvia could go on, the brother spoke in a husky growl. "I got a friend at work's got that Lou Gehrig disease," he said. "Started out just like Molly."

It was a relief to be able to give them relatively good news. "I'm certain Mrs. Simmons isn't suffering from ALS," Sylvia said, and the family seemed visibly relieved. She always found it useful to know what her patients feared. They worried about things they'd heard about on TV or on the internet, cancer or brain tumors or heart disease, but seldom considered Huntingdon's Chorea or Reiter's Syndrome, which in their own peculiar ways were worse. Sylvia's job was often that of educator, but her subject was always the horrific.

"And it's not that AIDS we're always hearing about, is it?" The way Mr. Simmons asked the question indicated this was his real fear. Sylvia shook her head no, wondering why he'd imagine his wife had a sexually transmitted disease.

"Absolutely not," Sylvia said, and she could feel the sigh of relief. Having gotten their fantasies out of the way, she slid the plastic film into the viewing screen on her office wall, hoping to explain or at least demonstrate some of the findings. "These solid areas are plaques," she said, indicating some murky gray areas. Mr. Simmons pulled glasses from the pocket of his work shirt and edged closer. She felt the brother's warm breath on her shoulder and moved slightly to the side. They both looked at her for further enlightenment.

"That's not normal," Sylvia said, making things as simple as possible. "It indicates some trauma to Mrs. Simmons' nervous system."

"Seems pretty calm most of the time," her brother observed. "She's got her issues, but mostly she ain't nervous."

Unintentional gallows humor was often part of the job. Sylvia suppressed a smile at the brother's use of the word issues. He might have heard it on Dr. Phil or Oprah, but Sylvia didn't want to pursue that. "I didn't mean that Mrs. Simmons is nervous," she continued. "Nervous system in this case doesn't refer to your emotional state. Everyone has a nervous system. It controls the brain and most of our bodily functions."

The Simmons' nodded in unison, not wishing to argue, intimidated by the film Sylvia had mounted on the wall. Mrs. Simmons had not yet spoken. "What's it mean then?" Mr. Simmons said.

"Unfortunately, I'm still not completely sure about that," Sylvia said, unwilling to commit herself until she knew exactly where she was going. "The nervous system is what's common; the plaques I showed you aren't."

"Not sure," Mr. Simmons exploded. "I'd like you to tell me something you *are* sure about for once. We're coming down here six weeks now. You're poking, examining driving my poor wife crazy. She's inside that goddamned tube for forty-five minutes scared out of her wits, and you still don't know why she's falling down in our kitchen. What kind of doctor are you anyway?"

"Not a very good one in your opinion, I'm sure," Sylvia said. But she was grateful for his anger. Why shouldn't he be outraged? Even if she knew that good health was a gift that people took for granted and assumed would last forever. She knew that whatever intellectual satisfaction she might take in working through this puzzle, it was ruining the Simmons' lives. "I do have some ideas," she said, trying to reassure them. "And the tests helped. I'm narrowing things down and getting closer to finding out what's wrong. I'm sorry I can't be more definite, really, I am."

Mr. Simmons' anger subsided as quickly as it had erupted. "It's okay," he said. "It ain't your fault, I know that. It's no one's fault. Thing is, for years she's just fine, waking up early, taking care of me and the kids, doing the laundry and housework. Then, before you know it, she's on her keyster, too tired to butter bread. Takes your breath away, I'll tell you, how quick it came."

"Diseases are often like that," Sylvia said, as much to herself as to Simmons. "They just appear for no apparent reason."

"But it's real, right?" the brother put in. "I read in the *Readers Digest* some people ain't really sick, even if they can't work and all."

"You're probably talking about Chronic Fatigue Syndome," Sylvia said. "Some things aren't imaginary, but can be a product of an emotional condition. But what Mrs. Simmons has is certainly real, I can guarantee that." It was important that they know this, that Mrs. Simmons have the support of her family. The last thing she needed was anyone thinking she was malingering. "In a few weeks I'll be able to tell you more, but I believe Mrs. Simmons has a neurological illness, which means her falling is unrelated to trauma or a tumor."

"She don't have cancer then?" Mr. Simmons said.

"No," Sylvia said patiently. "We've ruled that out." Who the "we" was exactly was uncertain, even to her. Dr. Peters, the referring physician was out of this now, and the faceless laboratory technicians who processed film were usually unable to interpret their own work. In reality, she was in this alone, trying to make it all understandable and somewhat less frightening for her patient.

For the first time, Mrs. Simmons spoke. "That's what I was worried about, that cancer, to tell the truth. I guess I can live with anything else."

"Okay," the brother said, summing up. "She don't have cancer and she don't have the AIDS or Lou Gehrig's?"

"Yes," Sylvia said, keeping things simple for the time being.

The family took this as good news. Mr. Simmons and his brother-in-law slapped palms and relaxed into their chairs. In a sense they were right, but given the range of diseases Mrs. Simmons might have, Sylvia was not encouraged. She often said in a joking way to friends, "If you come to see me, there's a good chance you're really sick." It was a bad joke, but true. Sometimes she hated how true it was. Now she allowed the Simmons' to think the worst had been ruled out because it was easier for her, and she was secretly ashamed of this.

"Well, all right then, Doctor," Mr. Simmons said. "I guess we'll be seeing you later."

Sylvia smiled in response, but there would come a time when she would have an answer for them and she was reasonably sure no one would be smiling then.

Sylvia had found a sealed letter from Mitchell on the breakfast table that morning, but hadn't had the time or will to read it. Now she took the single sheet out of the envelope and spread it before her on the desk. It seemed to be in response to their aborted talk about happiness, though Mitchell didn't address that directly. Instead, he had made a list, below the title: "What I Need From a Woman." Sylvia noted the indefinite article, and then she read what her husband had written.

1.) A willingness to share in my life and concerns.
'2.) Support for my work.
3.) To be a partner in every sense.
4.) A love of the natural world equal to my own.
5.) Sensitivity to the arts and literature.
6.) Commitment to social/political issues.
7.) Spirituality.

Sylvia went through the list carefully twice, noting that it was Mitchell's life, work, and politics that needed to be supported. Apparently the woman in question was to have no such need, or perhaps Sylvia was misunderstanding his intentions. Maybe the appropriate response would now be to supply Mitchell with a list in response. Then they could collate the two lists and negotiate a final document which each could sign, like a treaty or formal agreement.

She wasn't sure whether this list was a reaction to her question about happiness or something Mitchell had been thinking about for some time, a sort of declaration or demand for satisfaction. In either case, the whole thing seemed so pathetic as an attempt at communication that she wanted to laugh. It was obvious, however, that Mitchell expected some kind of response.

She sat back in her chair, wondering how they had gotten to this point, but she could identify nothing, no root cause, no developing problems that she might have attended to earlier. Their marriage hadn't started out this way. In the beginning they were at least able to talk to each other. Neither of them intended for things to develop as they had, but here they were. What was wrong with their marriage was idiopathic, like Mrs. Simmons' dizziness and Sylvia thought it had about as much chance of successful intervention. She looked again at the list and shook her head. Then she started arranging her things for the afternoon carpool. She checked her list of patients for the following day, and then, in the margin of her calendar, wrote: "Call lawyer."

CHAPTER SIX

Mitchell was quiet that evening, not mentioning the list he'd left for Sylvia nor asking what her response might be. Similarly, she said little beyond polite inquiries about his day, what they had for dinner, whether or not he'd rented a movie. In the end, she hadn't called a lawyer, though she knew good ones. She felt an obligation to let this play out as it might. Then when the kids were in bed and they were back on the porch with their cups of tea. She said, "Mitchell, we have a problem. A serious problem."

"Yes?" Mitchell said. He had been reading and seemed annoyed at the interruption. He had recently changed from bifocals to half-glasses and though he might have thought they made him appear more intellectual, he was having trouble adjusting to reading with them. Now he put the book down and looked at her. "Really, what is it?" He seemed to reserve to himself the right of escape should the conversation be burdensome or unpleasant. He was careful about such things.

Sylvia's immediate thought was that she'd like to strangle this man, to hold on to his turkey neck and just shake the goddamned thing for a while. "Yes. I think we should consider separating."

Mitchell seemed to regard this with the kind of interest he would devote to the opening of a new restaurant, but it had been no different the first time they separated. Then Sylvia had *wanted* him to protest, to fight her on it. Instead, he just left. Despite her frustration, however, Sylvia still felt responsible, as if she should have done more to work things out between them. "You're unhappy?" Mitchell said, apparently referring to their conversation the night before.

"Aren't you?" Sylvia said. "I read the list you left for me this morning. You sure don't sound happy to me."

Mitchell thought this over. He closed the book on his finger, an indication that he was taking this seriously. Obviously, this wasn't the response he'd hoped for or expected when he left the note for Sylvia. "I don't know," he said. "I don't think I'm particularly unhappy. That was more a kind of free writing, a wish list, if you want." Then, abruptly, "Are you in love with someone else?"

Which was the way he thought. Rather than accepting his share of the responsibility for what had gone wrong, Mitchell assumed it must be something outside of him, some interloper interfering with his contentment, which was just another reason the marriage was hopeless. Briefly, Sylvia wished there were someone else if only because it would make it easier for Mitchell to understand. "I'm not sure," she said, limning the truth. "Maybe."

Mitchell nodded. Now he put the book down but he still didn't seem upset. Sylvia had been afraid he would ask who it was or suggest they get into marriage counseling or express concern for the children. He might have fought her and said he wasn't giving up on the marriage. Sylvia would have welcome this and had rehearsed answers, but Mitchell just said, "I've noticed. I'll begin looking for a place tomorrow. There are vacancies down around the University. It would be convenient for me and not too far for the children."

Sylvia considered asking what Mitchell had noticed since he'd said nothing before, but she knew that whatever he might have said should really have been said years ago. It was sad but she found herself speechless as she often did with Mitchell, so she just turned and went to bed.

Mitchell slept on the sofa in his study that night, but Sylvia awoke at three and saw him standing at the foot of the bed looking down at her. In the fog of sleep she couldn't be sure what she'd seen, if he'd said anything or not. Later she wondered if he'd actually been there at all or if she'd imagined it. Neither of them mentioned it in the morning and by the end of the week, true to his word, Mitchell had found a furnished apartment and was gone.

Sylvia's immediate feeling was exhilaration. It was the most adventurous thing she'd ever done but her sense of triumph faded with the reality of lawyers childcare and what she imagined would be the outrage of his family. Mitchell's muted reaction to her request for a separation turned out to be only the beginning of what Sylvia would come to see as an extended campaign against her, carried out not just in his own family but among their friends and the larger community. Generally men were considered monsters in divorce situations and women victims, but in their case this was reversed, for reasons that were mysterious to Sylvia. A woman came up to her in the parking lot and accused her of flirting with her husband, a man Sylvia didn't even know. Then the woman said, "It's not enough you're destroying your family, you have to destroy others too."

People she had considered if not friends at least friendly acquaintances snubbed her when she was dropping the kids off at the JCC and once when she raised her voice calling Simon, one of the secretaries came out of the office and said, "Don't take out your personal problems on the children, doctor. It's not their fault." Sylvia remembered reading once that divorce was like death and she thought, yes, except in divorce no one says nice things about you.

Regardless of the unpleasantness she was experiencing around the divorce, however, Sylvia remained convinced she had done the right thing. She was grateful for having a job that demanded constant attention. At least during the day, this provided welcome release from the divorce proceedings.

After dropping the kids at school she spent the morning in her office seeing patients. Then she went to the University to conduct grand rounds. After discussing transient ischemic episodes with an earnest group of medical students, she visited a patient who had awakened with partial vision in one eye and was being worked up for stroke. He was a bald, over-weight man of 55 with small, determined eyes. Sylvia noticed with some surprise that on his chart that he was identified as a poet.

"This is it, isn't it, Doc," the man said.

Sylvia was behind the patient at the time, hidden by his bulk. "What, Mr. Marvin? This is what?"

"I had a stroke. I'm going to die, right? You can be honest with me."

"I don't think so," Sylvia said, wondering if she was being honest. "Not right away anyhow. Maybe later."

She intended levity so was grateful when the patient laughed, his slow growl coming through like thunder on her stethoscope. "Sure," he said. "We're all going sooner or later. But this isn't what you'd exactly call a good sign, am I right? I mean, this isn't really a very positive thing?"

Sylvia smiled. Intelligence was a rare gift among patients in her practice, as was humor. "No, I wouldn't say going blind is a good sign," she agreed. "You're right about that. But the thing is that in itself it's only a sign, nothing more. We have to figure out what it's telling us." She smiled in what she intended to be a hopeful way, then patted Mr. Marvin on the shoulder. " I'll see you tomorrow," she said and walked out of the room.

That was her morning. Now she was working her way through the maze of buildings at the Medical Center, looking for the bio-feedback center at the University. Her appointment was at three and she was running late, as usual. The director of the center was named Dr. Nygaard and Sylvia had a vague memory of him from residency but she never been here. Nygaard. had told her over the phone that he was located in the basement of the day care center which seemed like an odd location, but when Sylvia finally found the right building, the center was empty of children or staff and she descended the stairs with a mixture of anxiety and anticipation.

The ostensible reason for her visit was to consult with Nygaard about a patient with migraine headaches whom she had referred to him, but this could as easily have been done over the phone. Nygaard's specialty was pain management and though he had a national reputation, he was a psychologist and viewed with suspicion by the medical school. Which accounted for the out-of-the-way location of his office. Ironically, it was the fact that he was a pariah that had brought Sylvia here. She identified with Nygaard because both of them were outsiders. No one at the hospital had said anything directly, but separation and divorce made everyone uncomfortable. She imagined her colleagues and patients were all aware that Mitchell had moved out and taken a two-bedroom apartment. She had little doubt that women were already taking him covered dishes and casseroles.

In the dim light of the basement Sylvia walked hesitantly down the hallway, looking at the doors as she passed. At the end of the line was a sign she could barely read in the gloom:

Anders Nygaard. Knock First.

For some reason she read knackwurst for "knock first" which reminded her that she was hungry. The connection made her laugh
and she was still smiling when the door opened to reveal a stooped
man with thinning hair wearing a green visor that bisected his
forehead. He looked up, curious, as if visitors were infrequent but
not unwelcome."Yes?"

"Oh, God," Sylvia said. "I'm really sorry. Dr. Nygaard, I'm Sylvia
Rose. We had an appointment."

Nygaard smiled now, as if he wondered why she had been laughing but didn't want to ask. "Ah, yes," he said. "Dr. Rose." He looked
her up and down appraisingly. "Ah, I think I remember you from
medical school. You were one of ours, weren't you? Very bright, as
I recall. Many honors. Ah, yes."

Sylvia thought his speech patterns were odd, as if he had once
stammered and adopted the habit of saying "ah" as a strategy for
getting into a difficult word or sentence. She nodded. "I did both
medical school and my residency here. I always heard about you
but I never took one of your classes. I don't think we've ever met."

"Ah, yes," Nygaard said. "And so now we have." He waited,
apparently to see why she had come to see him in his basement
sanctuary.

This made Sylvia self-conscious. "I'm really sorry," she said again."
My husband just moved out and your sign struck me as funny."

Nygaard nodded as if this conjunction made sense. "Ah, yes.
The sign." He looked at it now, as if to understand his part in all
this. Then "Won't you come in?" He stood aside and gestured
toward a table piled high with journals and off-prints of articles.
Sylvia took one of the straight-backed chairs and Nygaard joined
her at the table. She noticed that contrary to her initial impression, he was tall and thin with a small brush moustache. His tie was

tucked into his shirt in military fashion and he wore short ankle boots, which irritated Sylvia for no good reason. Still, his gray eyes were intelligent and this had a calming effect on her. He laced his fingers together and leaned back in his chair. "You know, coincidentally, recently I saw one of your patients, a Mr. Mankwitz."

Sylvia shivered involuntarily. She felt as if this Moses were following her around, to her office, now even here. "He's not really my patient," she said quickly. It was a sore point because of the M&M but whatever she might think the rest of the world seemed to consider Mankwitz to be hers. "I'm a little surprised he came to see you."

"He had been in the ED and they noticed his pressure was elevated. Since I also do the blood pressure lab for the University, they sent him over." Nygaard hesitated. "An interesting man, but very nervous, hmm. He had his books with him. You know about his books of course."

"You mean the ones he brought down from Mount Sinai?"

Nygaard smiled but didn't laugh, as if he had learned to respect all opinions, no matter how unlikely. "Yes," he said. "Those."

"And did you help him; did he bring his pressure down?"

Nygaard shrugged. "In the lab we were successful, but that's not surprising. It's a controlled environment, completely unlike life outside. In order for the treatment to succeed, the patient needs to repeat the exercises over an extended period of time." He gestured toward the hallway. "Unfortunately, I doubt Mr.Mankwitz will be back. He seemed to think it was all a bit weird." He shifted in his chair as if to signal that this topic had been exhausted. "So, how can I help you, Dr. Rose?"

Help. It was a simple word, even a concept. They were in the helping professions, after all. Yet no one had offered Sylvia help for a long time, and without meaning or wanting to, she started to cry, tears leaking from her eyes and onto her black dress, as she looked directly at this strange man in his stranger place. "Damn," she said, because she hated this, hated the predictability of it, hated being the weak little woman crying on the first available shoulder, but she couldn't help it. She dabbed at her eyes with a handkerchief and said, "I'm sorry, Dr. Nygaard. I never do this. I'm just tired. Really, it's nothing."

Nygaard's expression gave away little. She didn't know if he believed her, but it didn't seem to concern him, and she found this comforting. She wondered if people often cried in his presence, and as a result he had learned to feel neither alarm nor surprise. He didn't repeat his offer of help but rather maintained a respectful silence, his small gray eyes unwavering. He didn't seem in the least embarrassed, and he didn't turn away. He waited.

Sylvia blew her nose and straightened in her chair. "I came to see you about another patient of mine," she said. "Mary Lindstrom. Do you remember Mrs. Lindstrom? I referred her to you. The woman with arthritic pain?" Sylvia had sent her patient to Nygaard because there was little else she could do for her. And while she didn't endorse the holistic approach in general, she wasn't opposed to alternative medicine, if it worked. Mrs. Lindstrom had been skeptical and only agreed to come because Nygaard was Swedish.

Nygaard nodded. He looked up at the ceiling and without thinking, Sylvia looked up too, as if his notes on the case were pasted on the soundproof tiles. "Mrs. Lindstrom," Nygaard said thoughtfully. "She did come in. Twice, in fact. But like Mr. Mankwitz, she had a reaction to the lab and so it was difficult to work with her. Some people have problems with biofeedback and also with me. It's kind of a Dr. Frankenstein thing, I think." Although the joke was on him, this seemed to please Nygaard inordinately. He smiled wickedly, a devil-may-care look that Sylvia supposed was intended to reassure her.

"What was the problem?" she asked. "With the lab, I mean. Maybe I can talk to her." Sylvia's offer was sincere but the basement office gave her the creeps too. She couldn't really blame Mrs. Lindstrom for feeling the same way.

Nygaard shrugged expressively. "I wouldn't bother trying to coax her in if I were you. The training isn't easy. People have to be willing to accept the treatment if it's going to have any chance for success. Some aren't, for a variety of reasons, and resistance just makes everything more difficult."

This seemed like a reasonable position to take. At the same time, Sylvia wondered how Nygaard held on to any regular patients with such a laissez faire attitude. Everyone she referred to him seemed to take a look around and run. Still, he didn't seem defensive. Perhaps because he really believed in what he was doing. For a moment they sat silently in their chairs, thinking of Mrs. Lindstrom. Then Nygaard said, "Perhaps you'd like to see for yourself?"

"What?" Sylvia said, imagining he had Mrs. Lindstrom sedated somewhere in the dark reaches of the basement.

"The lab," Nygaard said. "If you're going to refer people, wouldn't it be a good idea to know more about the treatment?" Without waiting for an answer, he rose and opened the office door. Then he gestured with his outstretched arm and Sylvia followed him down to the end of the dark hallway, where he unlocked another door and stood aside to let her enter. The hallway was empty; indeed the whole building was quiet. There seemed to be no other offices here except the deserted day care center upstairs. She hesitated for a moment, remembering the Dr. Frankenstein reference, but Nygaard seemed more comic than menacing in his green visor and ankle boots. She reassured herself that he was a professor on the medical school faculty. How dangerous could he be? Besides, she was feeling adventurous. "Excuse me," she said, and walked past Nygaard into the lab.

After the build-up, Dr. Nygaard's laboratory was somewhat disappointing, consisting only of two small rooms that communicated with each other through a large window. In the main room was a machine that looked oddly like three stereo receivers stacked one on top of the other. A desk and chair were next to these and blinking red lights gave the room the appearance of an airport controller's booth.

The adjoining room was smaller and furnished with a large recliner. Sylvia tried to hide her disappointment, but Nygaard was apparently inured to the reactions of others. He ducked his head modestly. "I know it doesn't look like much," he said. "But it's adequate for my work. I have everything here I need."

Sylvia had seen enough and now she was anxious to get back to her car. She thought she might have time for a cup of coffee before picking up the children. Still, courtesy demanded that she show minimal interest. She had gone to the trouble of coming here and Nygaard was right in saying that if she was going to make referrals she should at least know something about the treatment. "What exactly do you do in your lab?" she asked.

The question seemed to energize Nygaard, who answered with his peculiar hiccoughing speech. "Ah, yes, what *do* we do, that's the question, isn't it?" He laughed silently, amused with himself. "Ah, yes, well, I could explain, but it's much simpler just to show you. Please." He held out his hand again, gesturing toward the lounger and Sylvia sat, feeling unpleasantly small and vulnerable as the cushions gave way to accept her. Nygaard produced some headphones and placed them on her ears. He attached a blood pressure cuff to her right arm. Then he took conducting jelly from a jar and smeared some on her forehead and arms. Finally, he attached small rubber suction cups to her brow and forearms and connected these by wires to the headphones.

Nygaard inflated the cuff and then let it deflate slowly. "Your pressure's a bit high," he said, but when Sylvia started to protest, he nodded his head. "No worries," he said. "It's natural to be nervous at first and it's just a baseline reading." This was no doubt true, but it made Sylvia feel as if she were going to have a heart attack right here in this basement room with only the mad doctor to care for her. Maybe it had all finally gotten to her, she thought, Mitchell, the Moses, the myriad demands of each crazy day. Her mind was racing, but it was always hard for her to slow down and sitting here made it no easier. As if he intuited her thoughts, Nygaard patted Sylvia on the shoulder. "No worries," he repeated. "I'll be just a moment." Then he disappeared from the room, leaving her alone.

Sylvia wanted to scream. No worries indeed. Her husband had moved out, her children were climbing the walls, her practice was out of control. Despite her assurances to Luther, she had become over-involved with Thomas Morris and now having dropped his lawsuit against her, Mankwitz wanted to become her patient for real. Against all this, she found herself in a basement room with leads extending from every part of her body and Dr. Nygaard next door telling her not to worry. It seemed to Sylvia that all she had were worries. Things here had gone farther than she had intended, but now it seemed impossible to leave. She felt molded to the chair and was afraid she would electrocute herself if she tried to move. Given no choice, she sat back and almost immediately felt her limbs go heavy. It was a pleasant, even seductive sensation. It occurred to her that she might fall asleep right here; it had been weeks since she'd slept soundly and now she felt oddly secure and cared for in this strange place.

"Ah, yes," Nygaard's voice came through the headphones. Metallic, she thought, but not uncaring. "Just relax. In a moment you'll hear some clicks in the earphones when I start the program."

Sylvia heard crackling, but it seemed to actually be inside her head rather than in the headphones. It was hard now to separate herself from the sounds that seemed all around her and her arms had become incredibly heavy. Still, her primary feeling was not panic but of a warm security settling over her like a robe. She thought she had never sat in such a comfortable chair and felt herself sinking deeper into the cushion. Quick tappings followed the crackling originating strangely in her ears before traveling across her brain from one side to the other. These were succeeded by more tappings with greater intensity and rhythm than what had gone before. Then the sounds chased each other around inside her brain. Each set in turn faster and more insistent than those that had gone before, but the effect was exhilarating, and Sylvia understood that the sounds were actually tracking impulses in her brain. She was witnessing the kinetic shower of thought that assaulted her constantly, the processes she had always taken for granted if she thought about it at all.

This insight had the effect of making her strangely impressed with herself, with this thing that was happening. It was a kind of entrancement and, uncharacteristically, it forced Sylvia to slow down and marvel at it all, as if she had accomplished something, reached a new kind of awareness. This feeling persisted for an indeterminate period until Sylvia became aware of Nygaard's presence in the room. She wondered how long he had been there, and was suddenly embarrassed by her abandonment.

"Ah, yes," he said. "You heard those sounds, the tappings?"

There seemed to be no need to answer, so Sylvia just nodded.

"What we want to do," Nygaard said, suggesting that this would be a mutual effort, "is slow them down."

"Slow them?" The tapping had sounded like hail on a tin roof, rapid and furious. It had a life of its own. That was what was so amazing. "How?"

Nygaard sat in front of her on a stool. "I can show you some exercises," he said, as if she had already agreed to a course of treatment and in the process become his patient rather than a colleague. "Rapid response is associated with anxiety; slowing is associated with relaxation. Just as warmth is." Nygaard raised her manacled hand to her cheek in a surprisingly intimate gesture. "You see?"

Sylvia's fingertips were like brands from a fire, warm and comforting. She looked at Nygaard in astonishment; she was always cold, never warm, feet, hands, everything. The scientist was smiling at her slightly, though not in an unkind or mocking way. "That's incredible," she said. "Really, I had no idea."

"No one does," Nygaard said modestly. "Everyone over at the medical school thinks I'm a crackpot."

Sylvia started to object, but she knew that what he said was true. People there, her former teachers, referred to him as Dr. Strangelove. She was ashamed now that she had shared their misconceptions. She thought perhaps Nygaard was a genius, though she supposed the two weren't necessarily mutually exclusive. Now Nygaard broke into her thoughts. He re-inflated the cuff and then let it deflate. He nodded and said softly, "120 over 80. Perfect. And since you've been in the lab, your temperature has risen from 81 to 90 degrees. The temperature of your extremities, that is."

Extremities. An interesting word, though Nygaard could not have known her associations. Mitchell had called Sylvia a person of extremes, highs and lows, even hysterical. "Why is everything always so intense with you?" he'd asked repeatedly. But this wasn't what Nygaard meant. He was a scientist and spoke with precision. He was merely pointing out the obvious, that her fingertips were the extreme limits of her body. Now he sat at her feet, looking oddly young, his thin lips pressed together, a deep line of concentration cutting through the center of his forehead. Sylvia marveled at his self-confidence. Nothing in him seemed to question the truth of his conclusions or the curative value of his procedures, and Sylvia envied him this. Something had undeniably happened to her because of Nygaard's treatment. It was measurable: her blood pressure had dropped and her body temperature had increased. Moreover, the rat-tat-tatting in her brain was less. "It's slowing down," she said, as much to herself as to Nygaard.

"Ah, yes," Nygaard murmured. "You seem to be a good subject."

This pleased Sylvia inordinately, but then she thought of the time, her children, her life. "I've got to go," she said abruptly. "Can you unhook me?"

"Of course," Nygaard said, neither pleased nor displeased. "It's just a demonstration," he said diffidently. "If you want to come back sometime, I'll show you the exercises I was talking about."

At dinner, the kids were studiously quiet; despite their youth they were trying to make a point. No food fights, no tears, no distractions. They seemed to be saying, "You should think about what you're doing. You should look at yourself." Yet even though she agreed with them in the abstract, Sylvia couldn't help feeling exultant that Mitchell was gone. She had imagined she might feel abandoned, but in the event it was like leaning against an open door. However they might be acting now, she knew she had hurt the kids and that this was unavoidable. She also knew that this mattered; it was something she'd have to live with for the rest of her life. But she couldn't have cared less about their father.

Around nine the phone rang. Sylvia debated ignoring it and letting the machine pick up, but it might be a patient. She had given Mrs. Lindstrom her home number. It was Mitchell. "I think we really need to talk," he said, a wheezing sibilance leaking through the receiver.

"I don't need to talk," Sylvia said, and hung up.

Then she waited, wondering what she would do if he called back. It would represent more motivation than he had shown in five years, more urgency, and she knew she would welcome this. But she waited fifteen minutes and the phone did not ring. So that was how it would be, she thought, and discovered that except for the children she had no regrets about the separation. It seemed odd that fifteen years with a man could seem this unimportant, matter so little. She wondered if there was something wrong with her, if she was an unfeeling bitch or justified in her response. In any case, there was no point in denying the obvious. Besides, it was late. She turned the phone off and went upstairs to bed.

When Mrs. Lindstrom came in, Sylvia mentioned that she had met Dr. Nygaard, though she didn't tell her patient that she had been in his lab or submitted to a demonstration. The treatment had had an effect, however. For the past two days, Sylvia had been aware of unusual warmth in her hands and arms and she experienced a new feeling of contentment. She wouldn't have said she was happy exactly, but she felt at peace, a term she would previously have viewed with suspicion if applied to her. At first she told herself that it was simply getting Mitchell out the door, but she wondered if Nygaard's techniques actually worked.

"That guy's weird," Mrs. Lindstrom said now.

"In what way?" Sylvia said, trying to sound neutral.

Mrs. Lindstrom looked at her as if she were demented. "You saw him, right? That little moustache and the way his nose twitches like a bunny rabbit. Then that contraption he hooks you up to, them earphones, and all. You didn't think that was weird? I felt like it was something out of Alfred Hitchcock."

Sylvia smiled at the reference. Most of her patients had no idea who Hitchcock was but Mrs. Lindstrom watched televised reruns in the afternoon. "Maybe so, but did the treatment help you?" Sylvia asked. "Is the pain better?"

Mrs. Lindstrom hesitated before answering. She was a large woman with ludicrously swollen knees and ankles. Alone since her husband's death, she was trying to remain independent but her son and daughter-in-law wanted to place her in a nursing home, as much for their convenience as for her own good. They had all agreed that Sylvia would be the final arbiter of Mrs. Lindstrom's fate. "A little," she admitted. She was reluctant to praise someone as strange as Dr. Nygaard but equally unwilling to lie to Sylvia, whom she trusted. "I have to admit I'm getting around better than I was."

"If that's true, if he made the pain less intense, and you're able to walk more easily then maybe it doesn't matter quite so much if he's a bit unusual," Sylvia said. This made sense but Mrs. Lindstrom didn't seem to be buying it. Sylvia thought of laying it on the line for her: Look, lady, if you want to stay out of that nursing home, your kids want to put you in, I'd do everything possible to help myself. But when she spoke, Sylvia was more measured. "I can tell you he's harmless," she said. "There's nothing to be worried about if you go back to see him and there's nothing dangerous about his treatments."

"Oh, I ain't worried about that," Mrs. Lindstrom said. "I can take care of myself. I just don't like all that glue he puts on your forehead." She stopped for a moment, her face twisted in thought. "Can't you just give me something?"

"You said the pain medication I prescribed made you sleepy. We could try steroids but you wouldn't like the side effects." Sylvia shook her head. "I'm sorry but there's no cure for the kind of arthritis you have. I know it's hard."

Mrs. Lindstrom waved this off. She had no interest in explanations or sympathy. She had worked making blenders for thirty years before her hands stopped cooperating and she had to quit her job. "I know all that, okay?" she said, resigned. "I'll go back to Dr. Frankenstein then." She flexed her fingers. "It just don't seem like he's really like you, you know. More like some kind of witch doctor. I half expected the guy to do a rain dance or be wearing a grass skirt When I came in. But I've got to admit it hurts less than it did before. Weird."

There was a message from Mitchell on the machine and listening to it, Sylvia noticed that he cleared his throat three times in thirty seconds. In most people she might have assumed this was caused by anxiety but in Mitchell she knew it was only an affectation, the way he imagined sophisticated people talked. It was sad that he was still making himself up at thirty-eight, but she was determined to stop feeling responsible for his limitations. "Since you refuse to talk to me," he began and then cleared his throat. "I think perhaps we should meet with a third person, someone who is objective. I've a few names and will ring them up if you agree. Then I'll let you know when they have time and you can follow up directly."

It annoyed Sylvia when Mitchell used Britishisms he had picked up on his trips, not only because they never sounded like him, but because they didn't sound like anyone. It was as if he was imitating Ronald Colman in a 1940s movie. "Right," he said and cleared his throat with finality, signing off now. "I'll wait to hear from you then."

Sylvia shook her head. Proposing mediation was the most effort Mitchell had put into their marriage. She wondered if it would have made a difference if he'd done this earlier, but Mitchell would still be Mitchell, counselors or not. It would be pleasant to blame him, but the ineluctable truth was she was equally to blame for what had gone wrong, perhaps more than he was. And she knew that until recently their dislocation had suited her needs. If she had a husband who asked more of her, she might have been unable to finish medical school. Mitchell's inattention was a vital component to her success, though it seemed strange to think of it that way. Useful as he had been, however, she could no longer stand to be around him, much less live with him. She was glad he had left; it was what she had wished for.

Dr. Nygaard seemed interested but not surprised when Sylvia returned and told him that his treatments had alleviated some of Mrs.Lindstrom's pain. They both knew she didn't have to come down to his office to tell him this. "Ah, yes," he said. "Usually there's some improvement, at least at first."

"You mean it doesn't last?"

"Nothing lasts forever," Nygaard said and smiled. "Surely you of all people know that, Dr. Rose. Everything we do is palliative in the long run, isn't it? There are just new treatments, new approaches. Even in the short term, though, this work is only helpful if you continue in the lab."

"Well, good news then," Sylvia said. "She said she's coming back. She's going to call you." Sylvia wasn't sure why she was so invested in this relationship, but she was. She wanted to please Nygaard, to encourage him.

Nygaard seemed skeptical. He ran his hand over scalp and then shook his head. "Really? That's surprising. I didn't expect to see her again. She seemed put off by all this." He gestured at the disheveled office, the table piled high with papers. "I think she wanted me to have a nurse and perhaps wear a white coat, but where would I put a nurse in here, even if I thought I needed one?"

Sylvia laughed. "Patients find those things either frightening or reassuring, sometimes both." Then she said, "She did find you a little unusual. She said that."

This appeared to please Nygaard. He seemed curious about his effect on people. "Ah, yes? In what way?"

"Actually, she said you were weird."

Nygaard laughed out loud. "Ah, yes. Excellent," he said. "You see, the mad scientist, just as I told you. That's wonderful, superb. And yet you think she's coming back for more?"

Sylvia nodded. "I'm here, aren't I?"

Nygaard's eyes seemed to glow with new understanding. "Ah, yes," he said. "So you are." He waited a moment, then he said, "Shall we go into the lab."

Sylvia thought his manner was charming, even seductive. It was as if he had invited her to bed, though there was nothing remotely sexual about the man. This time there was no hesitation on her part. She wanted to feel that warmth, that heaviness again and took her seat in the lounge chair with alacrity. Then she waited impatiently while Nygaard attached the leads to her arms and forehead. Finally she was alone in the little room, waiting for contact with her most intimate impulses, the clicks and whirs of every thought .

"Everything okay?" she heard Nygaard say into the earphones.

Without turning around, she waved at him irritably, wanting to get on with it. It was her new drug, this thing. She closed her eyes and waited--the clicking was fast and furious and she rode the intensity of her brainwaves, inside them now, excited and stimulated by the excesses of thought. Then, almost imperceptibly at first, they began to slow, and she felt warmth spread through her fingers and forearms again. It seemed as if she had actually melted into the leather chair, but she wasn't the least bit concerned by this. She was one with the chair, the small room, the headphones, the metronomic clicking in her ears.

Eyes closed, she was aware of colors, red, green, gold. It was interesting that her brain waves should be colored; she hadn't expected that. Then there was only the occasional click in her ears and the creeping warmth in her fingers. She was in a cocoon, a womb, everything was all mixed-up together, nothing was or could be separated from anything else. She had no body, no extremities. It was all one; all her. The outside world was gone, all her cares and concerns; she was aware only of the slowed clicking and the all-enveloping warmth in her extremities. But, oddly, it was all extreme and without a center. She was vaguely aware of herself slipping away but this didn't alarm her either. She wasn't asleep or unconscious, just somewhere else, somewhere incredibly peaceful. The clicking had almost disappeared now. There was one click, another fainter one and silence, then another softer yet and more silence. After a long pause, there was another. And then at the last there was nothing.

CHAPTER SEVEN

Sylvia preferred taking call for her colleagues on holidays to spending the time alone or traveling somewhere and fighting the crowds. It gave her first choice for the rest of the year and the children were spending Christmas with Mitchell's family. The only problem was that because of the skeleton staff the clinic maintained during these periods, she became in effect a general practitioner and was sometimes forced to see patients suffering from diseases about which she had never known much and now barely remembered. Still, it seemed well within her area of expertise when the bell captain at Author's Inn called to say that one of their guests had collapsed in the lobby.

Despite the name, the hotel really had nothing to do with literature or writers but rather referred to a family with a pretentious forebear who owned a great deal of real estate in Denver. And while the managed care company didn't cover the hotel's guests, who presumably had their own insurance, they did have a contract for the hotel staff, which explained the call. "Collapsed?" Sylvia said now. "How?" The question seemed silly, even to her.

The bell captain was stymied by her question. How did someone collapse? "I don't know," he said reasonably. "He was just standing there holding his daughter's hand and then all of a sudden he was on the ground."

Sylvia grabbed a notepad and started making notes as she talked. "Okay," she said, speaking quickly even for her. "Who fell, who are we talking about?"

"Mr. Lewis," the bellman said. "He's supposed to be some heavy hitter from out east, a writer, or something. Anyway, he was over at the University for the week giving lectures and then he stayed over, for an extra night, to see his daughter, I guess."

"Lynford Lewis? The novelist?" Sylvia remembered vaguely reading about his visit in the *News*. She remembered only because like everyone else she knew, she had been both impressed and shocked by Lewis' books about doomed marriages and the evils of drink. Reading him, it seemed inevitable you would suffer the same fate even if you weren't married and never drank anything stronger than Coke. He had a way of making the horrific believable, even inevitable. She remembered being nearly psychotic after reading his last novel, *Bring in the Nightmares*. But a daughter? It was hard to think of Lewis with a family that would be willing to see him. And now he was on the floor in the hotel across the street from her office. The appropriate thing would have been to try to turf him to Denver Health, but likely he wasn't indigent and she had to admit she was becoming interested in the case.

"That's the one," the bell captain said. "He's lying in my lobby talking gobbledygook right now, and I'd like you to get him someplace else."

Sylvia remembered Lewis being from Boston or New York, she thought. "And he has his daughter with him?"

"He sure does. Cute little thing. Four or five years old. She's pretty upset."

"I'm not surprised," Sylvia said. "Where's his wife?"

"Beats me. I'm just guessing, but I think they're divorced. She dropped the kid off two days ago and we haven't seen her since."

Sylvia looked at what she had in front of her in her notebook. A middle-aged man, she guessed, though the bell captain hadn't given Lewis's age, who collapsed in a hotel lobby with his five year old daughter in attendance. Typical Christmas Eve. It had even started to snow, but she doubted anyone in the Lewis family was going to be singing Christmas carols. "Okay," she said, her voice taking on authority now. "You want him out of there as soon as possible, right? He's making the other guests uncomfortable."

"You got it, Doc. I already called an ambulance."

"Well, don't bring him here. We have no beds and we don't know what's wrong with him anyway. When the ambulance gets there, tell them to take Mr. Lewis to Crawford hospital. I'll call ahead and give some orders so he can be admitted, then I'll meet him over there. I don't want him in some ED. Meanwhile, try to find the little girl's mother and have her call me over at the hospital."

Sylvia was only on the courtesy staff at Crawford and seldom rounded there, but the hospital was convenient to the hotel, had space, and was discreet. Neither reporters nor ambulance chasing lawyers would be hanging around the lobby. Still, when she arrived at the hospital an hour later, Jack Adams, the hospital administrator was waiting for her. "Nice Christmas present for us, Sylvia," he said. "Thanks very much."

Sylvia had known Jack since medical school and liked him well enough, though as a rule she considered administrators to be the enemy. All they cared about was the hospital's image and getting paid. It wasn't the best formula for quality patient care. "I thought you'd be pleased," Sylvia said now. "He's a famous writer; it'll improve your image." Crawford was known, if it was known for anything, for catering to the wealthy, who went to Crawford for rest cures and plastic surgery.

"A famous writer with no wallet," Adams said.

Sylvia was surprised by this. Who didn't carry a wallet? Not that she assumed all writers were rich but Lynford Lewis was if not a household name, very well known and, as far as she knew successful. Depressing movies with major stars were made based on his books. There must have been money in that so where had it gone. She was aware of a hollow feeling in the pit of her stomach. "Maybe he lost it in the ambulance."

Adams shrugged. "When they brought him in he was wearing a Brooks Brothers suit and the only personal property he had was a VA card from a hospital in Boston. No wallet, no keys, no suitcase. This guy travels light."

Now Sylvia understood. "Let me guess. You called the VA and they told you that since you caught him, he's yours for the duration, right?"

"Exactly," Adams said. "So it's my duty to ask you how the hospital is going to be paid for the excellent care we're giving and will continue to give this indigent famous writer?"

Sylvia patted Adams on the shoulder. "And it's my duty as a physician to examine my patient whom I haven't even seen yet. We'll talk later, Jack."

When Sylvia got upstairs, however, Lynford Lewis was in no shape for conversation. The great man was semi-comatose, his gray hair and beard matted, his pitted nose red and angry. He was older than Sylvia had expected, perhaps sixty, and he looked older than that. Lewis' eyes darted to her when she approached his bedside, but they were unfocussed and he didn't speak beyond emitting a series of moans in which Sylvia recognized syllables, perhaps the beginnings of speech, but no words. Periodically, Lewis scratched his arms furiously as if something was crawling on him. His forearms were already bleeding slightly and if he kept this up, they'd have to put him in restraints. Since Lewis was awake, or appeared to be, Sylvia was obliged to try to speak with him.

"Mr. Lewis," she said. "I'm Dr. Rose. You've been taken from your hotel to Crawford hospital because you collapsed and lost consciousness. Do you understand what I'm saying to you?"

Lewis didn't respond directly but he swung his arm at the IV tower, causing the nurse to run to steady it. Sylvia leaned over his bed and looked into his eyes with a light. Then she checked his chart and glanced at the nurse.

"BP's 180 over 110," the woman said. "Pulse is 105."

"What have you got him on?" Sylvia asked looking at the IV.

"Just sugar and vitamins. We were waiting for you."

Sylvia nodded. It didn't take a genius to figure out this guy's problem. She had done a rotation in the VA when she was a resident and saw enough drunks there to know what the DTs looked like. "We've got to get that pressure down as soon as possible. Give him a double dose of Tranxene--make it every two hours instead of every four. Call me if his vitals don't come down. And if he doesn't stop scratching himself, put him in restraints until he comes around. Okay?" Without waiting for an answer she turned back to the bed. Lewis hadn't moved and she couldn't decide if he was conscious or not. "I'll look in later, Mr. Lewis," she said.

When she came out of the room, a young man was waiting at the nurses' station. He was of medium height, with a beard, but it was his large intense eyes that caught Sylvia's attention. She didn't think he was from Jack Adams' office. Without expecting it, she felt something move inside. To cover herself, she adopted a brisk tone of voice. "May I help you?" she asked.

The man smiled, embarrassed, and this transformed his face. "Yes," he said. "I mean, I guess so. I hope so."

His uncertainty made Sylvia smile in return. She waited for him to regain his composure. "I should introduce myself," the man said. "I'm Charlie Steinmetz. I teach at the University and I was Mr. Lewis' sponsor for the conference on contemporary writers. That's why he's here," he said in explanation.

"Well, you've done a great job, Professor Steinmetz." Sylvia smiled again to show she wasn't serious, but in a way she was.

Steinmetz laughed, embarrassed. "I know," he said. "The first thing they've asked me to do since I came here and the guest of honor collapses in his hotel. I guess I won't have to worry about getting tenure."

"He didn't exactly collapse," Sylvia said more gently.

"No?' Steinmetz looked confused.

"Mr. Lewis is suffering from delirium tremens. He's a drunk," Sylvia said, realizing how tough she sounded, how tough she wanted to sound. The current thinking, after all, was that alcoholism was a disease and that alcoholics couldn't help themselves. She didn't buy it, in part because she wanted to think people could affect their lives, but also because most of the patients she saw suffered from neurological illnesses and really had no control over their bodies. It might have been simplistic but in Sylvia's mind all an alcoholic had to do to alleviate his illness was stop putting the bottle to his lips. Even in the moment of thinking this, however, Sylvia regretted it. She remembered how helpless Lewis had looked in his hospital bed, tubes strapped to his arms.

"But he's sick," Steinmetz said.

"He's sick because he drank too much," Sylvia said. "And from the looks of him he's been drinking too much for a long time. Sylvia knew this was unsympathetic, perhaps even unfair, but she didn't care. Sympathy never did alcoholics any good. And long-term drunks like Lewis, who often smoked too, usually suffered from related problems with their hearts, livers, and circulatory systems. It was never pretty and all things considered dying from the DTs in an excellent private hospital might be a good way to go. She wondered, though, if part of her response was in an effort to distance Charlie Steinmetz and make him disapprove of her. For reasons she didn't completely understand she didn't want this man to like her too much. "I'm sorry," she said. "This isn't easy for anyone.

But maybe you could tell me how to contact his family, next of kin? I understand his daughter was with him, but I don't see her here now. And where's his wife?"

Steinmetz looked more physically uncomfortable than embarrassed, as if he bore personal responsibility for what he was going to say. "That's going to be a problem," he began. He ran his fingers through his hair. "Yeah, a big problem."

"Professor Steinmetz, I don't mean to be abrupt," Sylvia said. "But Mr. Lewis is in intensive care. What that means in medical terms is that his condition is life-threatening. If we can't get his vital signs back to normal he could die tonight. He's semi-comatose and unable to respond to simple questions or care for himself. I need to contact his family or someone responsible for him in order to make decisions about his care. Can you tell me why that seems to be a problem?"

Steinmetz jammed his hands into his pockets and looked at the ceiling. "This isn't a good situation," he said. "His wife, actually his ex-wife, left town when she heard Lyn had collapsed. I had just come to the hotel to pick them up, but she just took the little girl and drove away. She said she'd had enough."

Sylvia didn't find this particularly surprising. Being married to a writer who drank couldn't have been easy and alcoholics often tried the patience of those who were closest to them. "Okay," she said, "is there anyone else to call then? Other children, siblings?"

"Actually, I went to school with one of his daughters by another marriage," Steinmetz said. "I already called her in New York, but she said she didn't want to be involved either."

Involved, Sylvia thought. How could you not be involved with your father? Since when was that a choice one had the right to make? "How many previous marriages were there, I wonder."

"There are four other children, all daughters, and from what I know they've all cut themselves off from their father," Steinmetz said, not answering the question directly.

Sylvia liked the fact that he didn't romanticize this, that he was straightforward about it, so she provided the sentimentality. "It's kind of sad, isn't it," she said, looking at the tinsel decorating the nurses' station wishing everyone a merry Christmas. "A great writer alone in the drunk tank in a strange town on Christmas Eve. And no one will take his calls. Not exactly the view most people have of the literary life."

"It's not that unusual," Steinmetz said. "In fact when I last saw him he was matching a colleague drink for drink in the bar at two AM, and they both seemed to be fine, considering. Of course, this is different, being hospitalized, I mean."

"Are you a writer, Mr. Steinmetz?" Sylvia wanted to prolong the interview, wanted Steinmetz to laugh again, or just look at her with those eyes. She noticed that he was well dressed in the shabby genteel way of academics. He was wearing a nice tweed sports jacket and rust corduroys beneath his trench coat.

"Oh, I'm just starting out," Steinmetz said. "Only one novel. Nothing like Lyn Lewis. But then, there's no one like him."

Sylvia nodded, but she was impressed with Steinmetz' modesty. Plenty of people would go to dinner for years on the strength of one book. She knew her husband would, if he ever wrote a book. Perhaps Steinmetz was that rarest of things, a man with real confidence in himself, who didn't depend on the opinions of others to validate himself. It seemed unlikely, though, to meet someone like that by accident in a hospital on Christmas Eve. For no particular reason, she wondered if Steinmetz was Jewish and with as little evidence as that decided he was. "And he lives in Boston?" she continued, all business now.

"He's not from Boston," Steinmetz said, "but he's been there for some time. He teaches at various places for short periods or gives lectures, but I think he has a room in Cambridge. I've been trying to reach a mutual friend there."

It was surprising. From what little Sylvia knew of writers, they had comfortable lives, often sheltered by universities which were more tolerant of their idiosyncrasies than the outside world might be. Or perhaps they were supported by their publishers. She remembered reading about Fitzgerald and his editor, how Maxwell Perkins had taken the author's daughter in when Fitzgerald and his wife were incapacitated by drink and madness, making sure the girl went to Vassar. The idea that someone as prominent as Lynford Lewis would be living alone in a furnished room with no money, friends or family just seemed incredible.

But as she thought about it she realized that no matter how affected she had been by his books, Lewis was not really primarily a writer anymore; his real job was drinking, just like every other alcoholic. It was what he thought about from the time he got up in the morning until he went to bed at night. He would have to maintain a blood level to feel normal, or what he had come to consider normal. Everything else would be secondary. Family, friends, career. Sympathy and understanding would do nothing to change Lewis' condition. Some drunks were able to work and maintain their lives for years. But in the end they were all the same, regardless of pedigree: they were all hopeless and they all made suckers of those who loved them. Which went a long way toward explaining the reactions of Lewis' daughters to his present condition.

"I understand he has no money," Sylvia said now. "The hospital administrator told me Mr. Lewis doesn't even have a wallet."

Steinmetz nodded. "Amazing, isn't it? When I met him at the airport all he wanted me to do was buy him a drink. He could hardly stand up when he got off the plane. He just asked when he was getting paid."

Steinmetz seemed shocked and somewhat insulted by this, as if Lewis should have been looking forward to meeting him and having a literary conversation. Disillusionment was hard on everyone.

"The point," Sylvia said, "is who's responsible for Mr. Lewis now? Clearly, he's in no position to act in his own behalf or make decisions and you said his ex-wife left town."

"You mean responsible financially?"

"The bill needs to be paid eventually," Sylvia said. "But that's not really my concern. What's urgent right now is that someone has to give me permission to treat him and sign a consent form for treatment. Considering his condition, there could still be a crisis and then I'd have to give orders to the nurses."

Steinmetz looked as if he'd been stricken himself. "He doesn't have anyone," he said. "No family and I'm the only one here who knows him. God."

Sylvia waited a moment. Then she said, "Congratulations, Professor Steinmetz, you just became Lynford Lewis' guardian."

"Is that legal?" Steinmetz said.

Sylvia shrugged. "Probably not, but it will have to do," she said.

The snow continued and as Sylvia made her way out of the hospital parking lot, cars were sliding around the streets in a lazy uncontrolled ballet, occasionally nudging one another, but seemingly too graceful to cause serious damage. Sylvia wasn't a skillful driver, but she wasn't concerned as she navigated the streets in her Volvo. She even hoped someone would lose control and hit her car. Not so hard as to cause serious injury but enough to delay her so she would be unable to make it to the mediator's office, where Mitchell was waiting. She had agreed to meet on Christmas Day because they were all Jewish and she had no patients to see. But she would have been reluctant to go on any day, regardless of the season.

Although she and Mitchell had had little to say to one another for the past five years, during their separation he seemed to have been seized by a desire to talk endlessly about what had gone wrong between them, what should be done for the children, what their living arrangements should be, what property and furniture should logically go to whom and what to do about any number of things that never seemed to matter before. Paradoxically, what they never discussed was the chance of their getting back together. Moreover, in these sessions, whenever he began to talk, Mitchell would collapse in a paroxysm of sobs, and then Sylvia and the mediator would sit watching him cry or, alternatively, wail. "I'm sorry," he'd say. "I'm okay; I'll be all right in a moment."

Sylvia knew she should feel sympathetic or moved by his pain, especially since she knew it was real. In his own way Mitchell suffered terribly from the separation, especially with what he considered the embarrassment of it all. More than once he had said that no one in his family had ever been divorced and that his mother was suffering terribly, something Sylvia found hard to believe since the old lady had never shown the slightest kindness toward her.

Sylvia felt disgusted by Mitchell's public demonstrations of pathos. She wanted to tell him to get a grip, man up, something. She knew her reaction was in part a defense against her own feelings of loss and failure in the marriage, but her immediate reaction to him was to become irritated, which had reached its climax during the previous session when the mediator, a social worker named Sarah Jewel, reached out to touch Mitchell's shoulder and the two of them fell into an embrace, weeping together at the exquisite sadness of it all.

This had been too much for Sylvia. "I'll just leave you two alone," she said, rising and not intending to return. Yet now she was going back because by the terms of the contract she'd signed she was unable to cut off mediation unilaterally. Even if it seemed more like marriage counseling than a legal proceeding, she knew they had to agree on a proper end to their marriage just as they had on its beginning Whether or not Mitchell drove her crazy, she knew she owed him that and how she might feel about Ms. Jewel, this was preferable to going to court and leaving everything up to a judge.

Mitchell and Sarah were waiting when Sylvia arrived and Sylvia could tell from the small wrinkle in the center of Mitchell's forehead that something was bothering him. As soon as they were seated, he said, "I think we have to deal with what happened last time."

Mitchell always wanted to deal with things. It was a way of giving the appearance of directly confronting problems when in reality he was the most indirect person Sylvia knew. The purpose of the mediation, for example, was purportedly to sort out issues of property, custody and support. Mediation was supposed to help them avoid going to court and make divorce if not pleasant at least manageable. The brochure in Sarah's outer office laid all this out in detail. So far, however, all they had talked about in their mediation sessions were Mitchell's feelings of loss and abandonment.

"I think we should deal with dividing up marital property," she said. "Then we can deal with the kids and child support. Aren't those the kinds of things we're supposed to be talking about?"

Both Sarah and Mitchell looked away, apparently embarrassed by Sylvia's bluntness. It made Sylvia angry that Mitchell once again had succeeded in making her act like a bitch. After all, she wasn't the one who'd left. Sarah said, "That's certainly part of what we're here for, Sylvia, but I think Mitchell has a point. Your leaving last week was a very powerful thing to do and we need to explore your feelings about that."

Mitchell nodded vigorously. Powerful was one of his words. Yet nothing he ever said was truly powerful or had any real force for Sylvia. He would say he was "alive" to this or that powerful event, but he hadn't seemed either alive or powerful to her for years. And the things that moved her didn't seem to matter to him. Now he said, "It's just that I'm aware of some hostility here, Sylvia." It was spooky because Sylvia had just been thinking this, about being alive and how dishonest that was. But Mitchell's gray eyes were achingly sincere and free of irony.

She hoped he wasn't going to start crying again. To avoid this, she tried to sound matter-of-fact and not raise the level of tension in the room. "Well, we're getting divorced, after all."

"That doesn't mean there has to be unpleasantness," Sarah put in. "Mutual respect is vital."

Which, of course, was the problem. Sylvia didn't respect Mitchell, not as a man, not as her husband. It was all she could do at times to restrain her laughter at the things he said. She wondered if what Sarah said was true, that divorce shouldn't be unpleasant. Perhaps it was the exact opposite; perhaps divorce should be as unpleasant as possible. It could be a kind of litmus test of a couples' commitment to one another. For Sylvia knew that as awful as this process was it would be worse to remain married to Mitchell.

Even as she thought this the image of the man she had just met at the hospital came to mind. Charlie Steinmetz, whoever he was or would turn out to be. His eyes and his smile. She knew the dissolution of her marriage wasn't about anyone else, even if she had elided the answer when Mitchell asked her. But part of the urgency came from her relative youth, the possibility of another life after this one, the chance that she'd meet someone else, and now she had or she might have. She hadn't noticed whether or not Charlie was wearing a wedding ring, but then she hadn't looked. She didn't even care. She wanted to see him again. That was all; in the end, it was surprisingly simple.

Her mind snapped back into the present. She had to be disciplined about this. One thing at a time and as like figures in a frieze, Mitchell and Sarah were right where she had left them, leaning forward anxiously, fingers knit in earnestness, expectation ripe in their expressions. Without thinking about it consciously, Sylvia found she had made a decision.

"I'm sorry," she said. "Maybe unpleasantness is a problem for you. But this is very unpleasant for me and I'd think for you too. Divorce is an adversarial situation. I'm not enjoying this and if you are, Mitchell, you've got problems I never even imagined. So I'll come back here for two more sessions because I do think it would be better to try to work things out without going to court. But that's all."

She turned to Sarah. "As for dealing, all I want to deal with are the issues we discussed in the first place. We're not here for counseling, so you don't need to worry about my feelings. If you really want to know, however, my main feeling right now is frustration that this isn't moving faster. I want to get divorced, the sooner the better. If you can help us with that, fine. Otherwise, I'm hiring a lawyer to make it happen."

She knew she'd over-stated things but she wasn't sorry because she wanted to shake the others up. Neither Sarah nor Mitchell moved; they nodded in tandem, apparently thinking over what she had said. It occurred to her now that they were the ones here who acted like a married couple and she the professional who was trying to intervene in a bad dynamic.

Finally, Sarah Jewel said, "Well, then, one thing to talk about would be your practice. Is that all right with you?"

"What about it?" Sylvia said. Mitchell's affect had altered subtly. Now he seemed alert, interested.

Sarah moved some papers around on the table in front of her. "Normally, in situations like this, when the couple has been through a number of changes together and one is a professional, an attorney or a physician, there's a settlement based on the worth of the practice."

So for all the tears and rending of garments, it was going to come down to money. Sylvia had never thought about what her practice amounted to financially, but she supposed it was worth something. Still it irritated her that Mitchell would bring it up in this way, so indirectly and through a third party.

"I worked my ass off for fifteen years to establish a practice," Sylvia said now, keeping her voice level. "I borrowed money to go through medical school and residency and paid it back out of what I earned. What's all that got to do with Mitchell? And since when is he not considered a professional?"

Mitchell ignored this. "I supported you during all that," he said. "I took care of the kids when you were on call or in the hospital."

Now Sylvia turned on her husband. "Did it ever occur to you that they were your children, too? You weren't a hired nanny, for Christ's sake. Why should you expect compensation from me because you took care of your own children? Let's get real here, Mitchell."

Sarah intervened again. "Often, one spouse will neglect his career to help another establish him or herself." She looked again at the papers in front of her. "According to your income tax returns, your income last year was almost two hundred thousand dollars. Is that right?"

Sylvia ignored the question. They had the tax statements. There was not going to be any disagreement over the figures, but that wasn't the point. They were paying Sarah two hundred dollars an hour so Sylvia didn't see why she should apologize for her income. "I don't think Mitchell denied himself much," Sylvia said. "For the past twelve years, he's been living quite well and has family money that makes mine look like something a kid could earn at a lemonade stand. I'm damned if I understand why I should pay him off or give him proceeds from my practice. It would make more sense for him to pay me."

Mitchell was starting to squint and Sylvia thought this might be preparatory to another crying fit, but she wasn't going to give way on this. It made her mad that he would even ask. He was the great ascetic, devoted to art and culture and supposedly caring nothing for material things. She suddenly realized that he and Sarah had talked strategy before she ever walked in the room. "I don't think that's a very productive way to talk about it," Sarah said now.

"Maybe not," Sylvia said, rising. "Frankly, I don't give a shit. For all your crap about mutual respect this comes down to what all divorces are about: money." She got to her feet and looked Mitchell in the eye. "I have to admit I expected better from you, maybe because of your parents, maybe because I really believed what you were saying all these years about art and philosophy." She shook her head, surprised to find she was near tears herself. She took a deep breath and continued. "The only reason I'm still here, and I truly mean the only reason, is to try to make things easier, but this mediation is a joke. You two are joined at the hip, so like I said before, if we can't get this resolved in another two sessions, I'm cutting it off. See you kids later."

Outside in her car, Sylvia started to shake uncontrollably, though it wasn't very cold, and then the tears came, running down her cheeks like sap on a tree trunk. It wasn't so much grief as frustration. She felt relieved about what she had done even as she regretted how tough she had to become to do it. She wondered if there was a way for her to let some of that go, for herself, her children, her patients. It might have been a forlorn hope but once in a while she thought she should be able to take comfort in the protection of a man, even if that had never been her experience with Mitchell.

The snow continued through the night, making the city look as if it were insulated in cotton, muffling the inevitable morning traffic noises, making everything seem softer and gentler. Sylvia overslept and by the time she got the children to school and rounded at the hospital, it was nearly 10 o'clock. She was due at her office at eleven but she wanted to check on Lynford Lewis, particularly since she knew Jack Adams would be trying to find ways to discharge him. Christmas charity was one thing, but Christmas was over and no doubt there were wealthy dipsomaniacs who needed that bed.

As she entered the hospital, Sylvia caught a glimpse of herself in the hall mirror and hesitated. She was still slim and graceful with jet black hair and a small mouth, but now she detected a vertical line bisecting her forehead and she wondered if this was new, or if it might be a physical remnant of her marriage. She had always valued her youthful appearance, always flattered herself secretly thinking that she looked younger than her peers. She moved closer to the mirror, examining her face, still tight and otherwise free of wrinkles at thirty-five. She wet a forefinger and tried to smooth her forehead, but then she realized that people were watching and she hurried on to the ward.

At the nursing station, several of Lewis' books had been arranged with some care so that anyone coming off the elevator would notice them. Sylvia recognized two she had read and picked up a book of stories entitled *Thirteen Ways of Looking at Disaster.* On the back, a much younger Lewis with a neatly trimmed beard wearing an oxford-cloth shirt and tweed jacket looked out at her. The biographical note said he was a professor at a Midwestern university known for its creative writing program, but the book had been published ten years ago. The Lynford Lewis she'd met wouldn't last long in front of a class, even one full of aspiring writers. The note went on to say that he lived with his family and their dog Max. Sylvia wondered which marriage this referred to. She knew what had happened to his children but the ex-wives were probably spread across the country in his wake. Disaster seemed like a good word to describe the path Lewis' life had taken. "Are we starting a lending library?" she asked the nurse.

The woman rolled her eyes. "That professor from the University brought them in and made us put them up there," she said. "Supposedly that old drunk they brought in on Christmas Eve is some kind of famous writer."

Sylvia nodded. "The funny thing about that is it's true," she said. Then she went in search of her patient.

Lewis was out of intensive care now and in a semi-private room. He was sitting up in bed watching a game show when she came in. He wore pajamas that said "Merry Christmas" on the pocket, but otherwise he seemed completely unexceptional. "Mr. Lewis, I'm Dr. Rose," Sylvia said. It seemed odd to introduce herself since she had been caring for him for two days, but he wouldn't remember their conversation of the night before. In fact he probably wouldn't remember anything that had happened.

Lewis didn't respond. He was smoking and his face seemed set in a perpetual sneer. "When can I get out of here?" he said. "This place must cost $200 a day."

It was an odd way to thank someone for saving your life. "More than that, actually," Sylvia said. "But you're not paying for it. Anyway, I can't discharge you yet. You were a very sick man."

Lewis shrugged. "I've been sicker. Lots of times. Why didn't they take me to the VA?"

He might have shown some appreciation for the fact that anyone sent him anywhere, that Charlie Steinmetz had spent Christmas Day driving around in the snow and calling all of his relatives, none of whom showed the slightest interest in doing anything to help. Lewis might ask about his small daughter who had been with him when he collapsed and was probably terrified at the sight of her father passing out in the hotel lobby, or even about his estranged wife. But Lewis evinced curiosity about none of these people. He seemed neither self-conscious nor apologetic for having become in effect a ward of the public and this made Sylvia mad. "They did the best they could to take care of you," she said. "Why do you drink?"

The man just smiled. "Come on, Doc," he said. "Don't patronize me. Why do you breathe? That's why I drink. I like to put it in my mouth. I like the effect it has. I'd like a drink right now."

"Even after what happened? You almost died."

Lewis shrugged expressively. "But I didn't, did I? The miracle-workers of modern medicine brought me back to face another day, grateful and chastened by the experience, as I must inevitably be. But tell me, when did they start making pretty young girls like you

doctors?" He smiled wickedly, showing Sylvia his teeth. "I think I
need to get the DTs more often."

Sylvia ignored this and checked Lewis' chart. He was conscious,
if that was an improvement, and his blood pressure was within normal limits, but he was still weak. They were pushing fluids but he
needed nourishment and another couple of days in the hospital.
"I'm not checking you out of here until you have a plane ticket back
to wherever you came from and a ride to the airport," she said.

"That sounds like imprisonment," Lewis said. "Why can't I just
go back to the hotel?"

"Because you'd get drunk again and maybe die this time,"
Sylvia said. "You may not care about that, but I'm not taking responsibility for it. Besides, you're broke. How do you think you'd
pay for a hotel?"

Lewis yawned. "That boy at the University would figure
something out. Nice young man. They'd have me teach a class.
Something. Universities always have room in their budgets for itin-
erant famous writers, you know."

It irritated Sylvia that Lewis trivialized his talent this way. She
thought of Thomas Morris and what he'd lost. But however Lewis
might act, she felt she had to maintain a façade of professionalism.
"Have the professor get you a plane ticket then," Sylvia said, and
left the room.

Jack Adams was waiting in the hall. He looked anxious. "When can
we get him out?" he asked. "The man has no way to pay his bill. He
should have gone to Denver Health or the VA in the first place."

"But he didn't," Sylvia said. "You know the rules, Jack. You can't
refuse treatment to an indigent patient. It's illegal. You caught him so
he's yours. Anyway, I hope you don't think I'm getting paid for this."

This didn't seem to impress Adams. "I want him out tonight,"
the administrator said. Ironically, it was the same conversation
Sylvia had had with Lewis five minutes before.

"Sorry," Sylvia said. "He stays until he's well enough to go back to Boston."

"Boston?" It was as if she had said Bangladesh or the Yucatan. "That could be days; this isn't a welfare hospital, Sylvia."

"Too bad," she said. "But I'll tell you this. If you make any move to discharge him or transfer his care to another doctor who'll do what you want, I'll call a friend of mine at the *News* and tell her that your hospital is ready to throw one of our greatest novelists out into the snow."

"You'd do that?" Adams looked stricken. "But you're on our staff."

"Don't tempt me," Sylvia said.

Jack looked at her in an appraising way. "You know, Sylvia, from what I've heard, you've been having some problems with patients recently. I don't know why you're asking for more."

She guessed he was referring to the Moses, but Sylvia just smiled, determined not to let him intimidate her. There was certainly no danger of her getting over-involved with Lynford Lewis. The man was a degenerate. "Even psychotics deserve medical care in our great nation," she said. "If you discharged this man and he went back to his hotel, got drunk again and died don't you think we'd have an M&M on our hands right here at Crawford? Believe me when I tell you that my process notes would reflect the fact that I'm feeling pressure from you to discharge the patient before he's ready to leave. I doubt that you or your bosses would like that, Jack."

"I have to tell you,. Sylvia, you used to be a lot nicer when you were a medical student."

Sylvia smiled. The man was right. "Sorry, Jack. I've been going through a tough time lately, but it doesn't have anything to do with this. I mean what I say."

"Okay, okay, don't get excited," Adams said. "I'm not saying we'll discharge him against medical advice. But I don't see why we're catching welfare cases."

"I'm not excited," Sylvia said, though her hands were shaking in her pockets. "I'm just telling you the facts of the case. Have a nice day."

There was a message waiting from Mitchell that made Sylvia grateful for voice-mail. She wouldn't have wanted some gum-chewing operator at an answering service to hear it. Mitchell might not be embarrassed by his behavior, but she was embarrassed for him. There was enough feeling left between them for that, even if it was primarily nostalgia for a shared youth. Sounding aggrieved, Mitchell said he hadn't appreciated her leaving the session with the mediator so abruptly. He wanted to make another appointment and Sylvia realized instinctively that this would go as the last one had and decided on the spot that despite what she had said, she wasn't going back.

Mitchell didn't really care about the fact that they were going to divorce, that they had lost whatever love had once held them together, and he didn't seem to be thinking about the effect all this had on the children. He was only worried about process, the manner in which all this would be accomplished, and how it might look to others. He wanted everyone to be comfortable with the eventual result and he didn't appreciate it that Sylvia wouldn't dance this dance. Without having thought about it deeply before, Sylvia now knew people didn't decide to split up because they respected one another but rather because they could no longer stand to be together.

She called Mitchell and left a message to this effect. Then, invigorated by her decision, looked at the list of patients she had for the rest of the day. Mrs. Simmons was coming in at three and Sylvia smiled at the thought of her truculent husband standing ready to protect her. Mr. Simmons would be no one's idea of an ideal man but he was far superior to Mitchell.

By the time she got back to Crawford, the snow was blue in the evening light and the ward seemed warm and hospitable. Jack Adams was in the vestibule and Sylvia began to think he was stalking her. "I turfed Lewis to the VA," Adams said jubilantly before Sylvia could greet him.

This was unusual because hospital protocol dictated that whatever hospital admitted a patient was responsible for the duration of his stay, whether he could pay or not. Despite her principles, Sylvia felt a sneaky admiration for the man's ingenuity. "And how exactly did you manage that?"

Adams smiled proudly. "I just told them what you said to me, that if they wouldn't take him, we'd tell the papers they were refusing to admit a famous novelist who was a war hero. I admit I exaggerated his war experience a little. He's too young for Korea and spent most of his service in Fort Benning."

Sylvia was amused. She had underrated Adams. "And you have your own contacts at the papers, Jack?"

"I don't even read them, except online. But the VA doesn't know that. Anyway, it worked. We're moving him as soon as you sign off on the discharge."

Which meant Sylvia would be off the case, except that she couldn't do it, even if it would be the easiest thing. "I'm not signing anything," she said. "The man has a life-threatening condition and isn't fit to be moved. You should know that and so should whomever you talked to at the VA. He's my patient and I'm not letting him go anywhere. Unless, of course, you want to move him against medical advice, and if you do, I'm writing you up.?"

Adams had a pained look on his face. "Sylvia, be reasonable," he said. "They treat drunks all the time over there. They know what to do with them better than we do."

"They handle poor drunks," she said. "Your service is limited to the wealthy ones." Then she left the administrator and walked down the hall to Lewis' room. He was sitting up in a chair, dressed and seemingly alert. "Get back in bed, Mr. Lewis," Sylvia said. "I'm not discharging you yet."

Lewis looked surprised, which pleased her. "I heard I was going over to the drunk tank at the VA. That's good enough for me."

"Well, it's not good enough for me," Sylvia said. And I'm your doctor, whether you like it or not."

Lewis hesitated for a moment, but then he started undressing. "I think maybe I like it," he said. "A kick-ass doctor and a pretty one at that. Interesting." He got back into bed and pulled the covers up to his chin.

Despite herself, Sylvia smiled. It was interesting that Lewis would describe himself as a drunk. Give him credit for self-awareness. Her previous experience had been with so-called social drinkers who had problems but wouldn't acknowledge them. To Lewis, it didn't seem to carry value, good or bad. It simply was as he had said normal as breathing and he was unashamed. She doubted he would have considered alcoholism to be an illness. It was something else, a choice, maybe a style of life. His honesty about this piqued her curiosity and she found she wanted to prolong the conversation.

She took a chair next to his bed. She had already given orders to the nurses; all they could do now was watch him. "Doesn't drinking get in the way of your writing?" she asked, just to say something. She had surprised herself with her reaction to Adams' attempt to outwit her by sending Lewis to the VA.

"Sure it does," he said, Lewis said with a lazy smile. "But not as much as having children. I always said I lost a book for every kid. Four kids, four books. That's a lot of money." He looked thoughtful for a moment. "Maybe I would have written a couple more if I didn't drink. No question I lost some time in hospitals over the years. On the other hand, what would I write about if I didn't have this? They'd probably be terrible books."

"So your books really are your life?"

Sylvia expected an ironic comeback, but Lewis seemed thoughtful. "Something like that. Maybe the other way around." Suddenly courtly and charming, Lewis smiled as he had on the book jacket, and said. "Thank you for asking, Doctor. Finding me the way you did, it must have been hard to believe I could be *that* Lynford Lewis."

"I have a good imagination," Sylvia said. "And there were the book jackets."

Lewis smiled again. "Of course, the professor vouched for me, Mr. Steinmetz."

"He was helpful too," Sylvia said, liking Lewis more than she wanted to. She shook his hand. "I've got to go," she said. "I'll look in on you later."

Outside, the length of the day hit her and suddenly her legs felt weak. She realized that beyond medicine, her intervention with Jack Adams on Lewis' behalf had been a kind of mediation. It was true that she had to advocate for her patient, but she also represented the hospital and the medical staff. What's more there were her other patients, her children and the genteel war she was carrying on with Mitchell. Still, she was pleased with this part of what she had done and that was enough for today. She was about to leave when Charlie Steinmetz appeared at the nurse's station like an apparition and she wondered if he had been there all along. He looked relieved, as if he had gotten some rest.

"I heard you stopped them from transferring Lyn to the VA," he said. "That's great. He doesn't look to me like he's in shape to travel." He hesitated as if there was something else on his mind, but then he shook his head, as if to drive it away. "I just wanted to thank you for all you've done," he said.

Sylvia was pleased to see him again, but praise made her self-conscious. "It was only what any physician would do for a patient," she said, which wasn't exactly true but true enough. "And, considering all he's been through, Mr. Lewis has some impressive strengths. Are you still his guardian?"

Steinmetz smiled quickly. "His daughter came through in the end, thank God. So I'm off the case."

There was an awkward pause and Sylvia realized that Steinmetz was having trouble saying what he had actually come to say. "Do doctors ever go out?" he asked at last.

This amused her, but she understood. The larger community considered doctors to be like priests in the sense that they were authority figures, who were presumed to have immense power. Her patients seemed to consider doctors to be inheritors of the world's sorrows and were surprised to discover they also had personal lives. Paradoxically, it was also the reason people became so angry with her. The expectations were unrealistic to begin with. "I guess they do," she said. "Sometimes. Do professors?"

Steinmetz flushed. "I'm sorry," he said. "I'm not good at this. I was wondering if you'd like to have coffee sometime, but I should tell you that I'm married, that is, I was. I'm getting separated."

The natural thing would have been to say that she was in the same situation, but Sylvia withheld this; she didn't feel like talking about it now. She wondered how precise Charlie's language was, if like Mitchell he was a man of process. He was getting separated, then he would be separated, then whatever would come after that would happen? But this wasn't really fair. She didn't know either Steinmetz or his wife and her suspicions probably had nothing to do with reality. It was just the way people talked. They were getting ready to do this or that when they were actually doing it as they spoke.

She decided to give Charlie the benefit of the doubt. She liked the fact that asking her had been difficult for him. She also liked the way he had taken responsibility for a writer whom he admired but didn't really know. A man had needed help and Charlie helped him. That was a good enough definition of character for Sylvia. "I'd like that," she said. She took a card from her purse and wrote her home number on the back. "You can usually reach me at one of those places," she said.

Then she walked out of the hospital into the snow, going back to the life she had been living which would now be different. Life was movement. Eventually, she and Mitchell would be divorced and Lynford Lewis would be discharged and go back to Boston, where he would no doubt repeat the process she had just witnessed. Finally, at some future time, he would succeed in drinking himself to death and she'd read about it in the newspapers, perhaps in one of those "Where are they now?' features. But she couldn't change that; it was one of the necessary inevitabilities you accepted when you cared for patients who were seriously ill. Sylvia cared about her patients but she knew she couldn't save them.

Now they all appeared before her as in a Greek chorus: Thomas Morris with his ruined career and useless limbs; Mrs. Simmons terrified that her dizziness would be as serious as Sylvia knew it was; even the Moses, confused about his mission to save the world, and unable to find the way to sanity; Mr. Whitley and Dr. Nygaard. They were all with her all the time along with the myriad patients whom she had treated at various times in various places in the past, all evidence of her commitment and ultimately her powerlessness in the face of mortality. It was necessary to block this out to care adequately for the patient in front of her, to focus, but in other undefended times, walking down the street or eating lunch in a restaurant the hopelessness of real treatment would flood in on her and fill her with despair. Not for the first time, Sylvia thought, it was a sobering thing to be a doctor.

As she walked toward the parking lot, picking her steps delicately to avoid ice and snow, she was aware of Charlie Steinmetz watching her from the lobby; she could almost feel his eyes on her back. But that was all right. She was interested in what this new thing would be, what it would become if it became anything. For the first time in a long while, Sylvia Rose was observing herself with interest and anticipation.

CHAPTER EIGHT

With Charlie Steinmetz' help Sylvia had managed to get Lynford Lewis out of the hospital and on a plane to Boston early that morning but already she was wondering if she'd been fair to the man, if she were too harsh, doubting as she did that his alcoholism was really an illness rather than a character flaw. Maybe her own biases had affected her treatment of the patient, though Lewis didn't seem to care. At the airport he'd been gallant leaning over her hand and then winking as he said, "Until we meet again, doctor. As we surely will." And then he was gone.

So her adventure with a famous writer was over, even if Sylvia continued to replay the case in her mind. She had learned early in life to distrust appearances and she was prone to second-guessing herself. Things were seldom what they seemed at first glance and this was as true of emotions as events. If she were anxious about money, it might be the result of some childhood trauma, like her father having disapproved of her and withholding rewards; if she were worried about catastrophic illness--in medical school she had nearly died from a dozen imagined maladies--it was because she was afraid to face a new task.

Had Freud made his famous comment in her hearing, she would have corrected him: "No, Dr. Freud. A cigar is never just a cigar." Life, unlike illness, could never be idiopathic, without an explanation. Sylvia knew she was inclined to think too much, to look for causes where they might be elusive, but she couldn't help being who she was. In her life, there would always hidden paths to the source, even if they remained undetected.

Whether this was true and regardless of her handling of Lewis, she had to put all this aside now and concentrate on the new case before her. She had a forty-five year old man in her examining room complaining of back pain with no apparent cause but which was so severe he walked hunched over and said he couldn't work. Sylvia had taken a rudimentary history, though Tom Chapin was not really her patient, just someone she had caught in the clinic. He had recently moved to the city and she was on his insurance company's panel. It was Friday morning and the man was grimacing in pain.

"Look, Doc," he said. "All I want you to do is renew my prescription. My doctor's out of the office on vacation and I don't live in Kentucky anymore. Either give me enough pills to make it through the weekend, or send me to someone in pain management who will."

Sylvia sighed. Everything had to be managed now. Care, pain, time. She needed grief management, but insurance would never cover that. Furthermore, she didn't even have a firm idea what she would be grieving, only that she felt continually exhausted and the world increasingly appeared to her in various tones of gray. But that wasn't Chapin's fault.

"Mr. Chapin, I understand your problem, but I don't give prescriptions to people who aren't my patients. It's Friday and you just walked in off the street. Your doctor should have given you enough pills to cover his vacation, especially if you were leaving the state. I'm sorry."

The man's face clouded with anger. "You don't believe I'm sick? Look at me, for Christ's sake. I can't even stand up. You can see that, can't you?"

"It isn't that I don't believe you," Sylvia said, though in a way it was this. People offered all manner of excuses for their behavior and often their explanations had little to do with the truth. In any case, she couldn't afford to trust her impressions alone. "I have to observe you, take some tests and try to arrive at an explanation for your pain before I can treat it. You're talking about some pretty serious medication. Narcotics."

"They already done all the tests back home," the man said miserably. "No one knows what the hell's going on. I can't work, can't sleep, can't do a goddamned thing."

Sylvia nodded in what she meant to be a sympathetic way but she wasn't sure she was pulling it off. She tried to focus on this patient. The pain could be idiopathic, some kind of infection that had struck with no obvious cause. It happened. But it was more common that patients on these kinds of narcotics shuttled between doctors trying to stockpile drugs, claiming their physicians were out of town or that they had lost their pills. It was the medical equivalent of the dog eating your homework, but much more serious. Sylvia couldn't just dole out narcotics on that basis, even if it meant occasionally an honest person was denied the help he really needed. "I am sorry," she repeated.

After the tension she'd felt during his birthday lunch, Sylvia had worried that she wouldn't see her father-in-law again, but Gregory surprised her by calling the day before and inviting her to lunch. "I miss you," he said simply.

"You've grown accustomed to my face?" Sylvia said hopefully.

"Actually, the whole package," Gregory replied.

Now she waited for him in their usual place, under huge shade trees that Sylvia liked to feel sheltered her from those things she was reluctant to face. Then he was there, leaning into her and brushing her cheek with his lips. "Sorry I'm late," Gregory said.

"You're not," Sylvia said. "I'm early." Late for everything else, she was always on time to meet Gregory, afraid he'd leave if she ever made him wait. "How are you?"

"Let's skip that part," he said. "I'm the same." He ordered an Arnold Palmer and then leaned back in his chair to look at her. "So you did it," he said finally.

Sylvia nodded. "Actually, we did it," she said. "Both of us."

"Sure," Gregory said, "but really, you did. I mean do you honestly feel that Mitch would have left you first. He's never taken the initiative on anything in his life."

It was an odd way for him to speak of his son, even if it was true. "Maybe not," Sylvia said. "But something had to change, I mean, change radically. I tried to tell Mitchell that but I guess I wasn't very good at explaining myself."

"I doubt that," Gregory said.

They ordered salads and talked about the kids, Simon's bar mitzvah, the passage of time. Then Gregory shifted in his chair and reached over to take Sylvia's hand. "I want to ask you a serious question," he said. "Do you think I've been happy in my marriage?"

"It's a cliché," Sylvia said, "but I think you've been married to your work more than to Martha."

Gregory smiled. "That wouldn't be wrong," he said. "Maybe I retreated into it because there were things in life I didn't want to face. You're too polite to say so but I wasn't much of a father either, never took the time."

He held up his hand to forestall objections but Sylvia wasn't going to offer any. Gregory routinely went to his lab on Sundays and holidays in addition to the 70-hour work weeks that were routine. She knew he was closer to his research assistants than to his family and in the weeks leading up to his annual grant renewal they seldom saw him at all. "You made some important contributions," she said. "Maybe it was worth it to you."

He nodded. "Maybe," he said. "My point is marriage is never ideal; as far as I'm concerned it isn't supposed to be. It's a way for society to organize us, sort us maybe, put you here, me there, someone else somewhere else. Not a very efficient way to do it but it's been around a long time in a lot of different societies. I doubt my parents were happily married either. I don't really think it matters very much."

Sylvia thought of her own parents. With all their flaws, they were still devoted to each other after thirty-five years. "I guess I think it does matter," she said. "Otherwise, I wouldn't be getting a divorce. It's too hard, on me, on the kids."

"And on Mitch?"

She nodded. "Yes, I'm sorry. I know it's hard on Mitchell too. Probably we never should have gotten married but we did and now we're both young enough to make another start."

"Have you got someone in mind then?" Gregory was leaning forward now, showing more interest than he usually did.

Sylvia thought of Charlie Steinmetz but there was a limit on how candid she wanted to be with her father-in-law, at least for the present. "No," she said. "I may not get married again."

Gregory didn't agree or disagree. He just sat back again, taking all this in. He took another bite of salad and drank some water. Then he said, "I asked you to lunch because I wanted you to know that we can still go on seeing each other. I was surprised to hear you were divorcing Mitch, but the truth is I wouldn't have married him either. I always thought he was over-matched with you. It sounds awful but it's true. Anyway, Martha may feel differently, but as far as I'm concerned we're still involved, whatever that means."

Sylvia smiled and took his hand. "I don't care what it means," she said. "I'm just glad to hear you feel that way."

Sylvia hadn't cooked a real meal in months, certainly not since her husband had left, but she still valued the ritual of putting hot food on the table and sitting with the children while they ate it. She enjoyed watching Simon attack his hot dogs with the abandon of a boy who had never been denied anything nor even suspected there might be a limit to whatever the world would give him. Now as she poured noodles into a bowl and tore open the bag of cheese, she tried to imagine the lot of women before processed foods and microwave ovens were invented. Life before mac and cheese and Hamburger Helper. Of course women didn't work then, at least women of her class hadn't, but that didn't change the fact that the ordinary tasks of life threatened to overwhelm her daily. A pillow sat abandoned on the floor as it had for weeks and she couldn't muster the energy to pick it up; papers, some no doubt important, covered every available surface; framed pictures sat on the floor beneath the spots where they would someday be hung if she ever got around to it. Never neat, the divorce had accentuated Sylvia's tendency toward slovenliness, and though she regretted it, there was seemingly nothing she could do to change. She had read in one of the women's magazines in the clinic waiting room that people were either neat or clean, but she seemed to be neither. It was all too much for her. She went into the other room to call the children.

Almost immediately after the separation, Simon had moved into the vacant seat at the head of the table, though his imitation of Mitchell was limited to ordering his sister around. Now they each recited in turn the events of the day in a singsong monotone that Sylvia nevertheless treasured. She tried to draw them out, encouraging them to elaborate on this class or that, to tell what the teacher had said about Abraham Lincoln or multiplication, but finally they sat silently in front of the food until Simon said in a soft voice, "Are you getting married again, Mommy?"

It was the same question his grandfather had asked but the way Simon phrased the question broke her heart, as if this separation and the inevitable divorce to follow were only part of a series of couplings to be repeated endlessly until they were finally old enough to go and live on their own, free from the bad promises of their parents. "I don't know," Sylvia said, realizing that she didn't. "I'm not sure anyone will want to marry me."

"You're pretty," Becky said defiantly, as if someone had attacked her mother.

"And you're rich," Simon put in.

Sylvia smiled. "Who told you that?"

Simon shrugged. "Tommy Billups says all doctors are rich. His dad said so."

George Billups was their neighbor and hadn't spoken to Sylvia since Mitchell moved out. It was disappointing, though she didn't really care about George. She was disappointed in him as a man. She thought he might have come over and offered to mow the lawn or wash storm windows and check the boiler. Something chivalrous and old fashioned. He could have taken Simon to a ballgame. It was hard to live in a fallen world. Still, rich? Where would that have come from? She would admit she was sometimes extravagant, that she had expensive habits when it came to personal grooming and clothes, but that was about all. No second homes or ski vacations for her. It seemed odd that George would say this.

"We're not rich, Simon," she said simply. She thought of the aging Volvo with the slipping clutch and wondered guiltily if she *should* be rich, if she would be if she were better with money. She had left all that to Mitchell, thinking it would emasculate him further if she were to take charge of their finances. Now she regretted this, along with so many other things about her marriage. Still, she didn't want to mislead or worry her son. "But we're not poor either. I guess we're rich enough," she said simply.

"Then why wouldn't someone marry you?" The boy seemed genuinely anxious, not theatrical.

Sylvia looked at the children reflected in the dark wood of the dining room table and considered the question. Many men would be reluctant to marry a woman with small children, but she didn't want to say that. Maybe it would be her choice. It was possible that she just wouldn't meet anyone; she might never fall in love. She hadn't been in love with Mitchell and it had taken her twelve years to realize it. She didn't want to make that mistake again. If she didn't fall romantically, crazily in love, she might well not chance marriage."I don't know. Right now, I'm just happy to be with the two of you."

A week later, Sylvia received a registered letter from a case manager in Phoenix. At the top of the page was written: "In RE: Thomas Chapin." Sylvia had to think for a moment, then she remembered. Chapin was the man with back pain whom she'd seen in the clinic. According to the letter, he had filed a complaint against her and asked to be referred to a pain specialist. The complaint said she'd refused him "appropriate pharmaceutical treatment."

Sylvia dialed the number on the letter and waited through the interminable clicking and Beatles medleys until the case manager came on the line. "Thanks for calling back, Doctor," she said. "Just wanted to give you some feedback. At Goodfeelings we think that's real important."

Sylvia guessed she was supposed to agree with this but it had been a long day and she wasn't in the mood for feedback. "What exactly was the complaint? That I didn't give Mr. Chapin drugs?"

"Oh, my, no," the case manager said. "Nothing like that, I'm sure."

"Because it's true," Sylvia said. "He wanted me to refill his Vicodan and Percoset and I refused."

She heard a sharp exhale and when the woman spoke, the folksy twang was gone. "Patient says you were unsympathetic," she said.

Sylvia had noticed that definite articles were the first to go in these cases. She was doctor and Chapin was patient. She sighed and the case manager continued. "Patient says he came into your clinic in pain after moving to Denver from Kentucky and you wouldn't treat him."

"It was mid-day on a Friday," Sylvia replied. "I had never seen this patient before and he appeared in my office unannounced asking for narcotics. I'm sure you can understand that no responsible physician would have given them to him. For all we know he's a drug addict."

"Are you accusing Mr. Chapin of being a substance abuser," the woman said in an arch tone.

Addiction was different than abusing something. Sylvia didn't think the man was actively doing anything to drugs, but she decided not to try to enlighten the case manager. "I'm not accusing anyone of anything," Sylvia said. "I'm just telling you how the world is these days. Mr. Chapin probably was in pain; I'm not questioning that. And it's possible I seemed unsympathetic, but my sympathy doesn't extend to prescribing drugs for people I don't know, whether they're in pain or not. If he was addicted, he may have gotten that way because another physician wasn't as careful as he should have been in dispensing narcotics, which as you know are very addictive. I don't know about that because I don't know Mr. Chapin. I do know that patients hoard drugs all the time and use them for various purposes, including resale and suicide. Does that surprise you?"

The case manager wasn't going to be drawn into an argument. Her job was done. "Just wanted to give you that feedback," she said airily. "Now you have a great day."

The phone went dead in her hand and Sylvia thought of the woman's closing wish. A great day? She should only hope for such a thing to happen in her lifetime. It had all started ten or fifteen years ago when people in restaurants and stores had started saying,

"Have a pleasant evening," when you paid your check, or "Have a good day," when you stopped for coffee in the morning on the way to work. Sylvia, for reasons of her own, had always taken this not as a mindless pleasantry but rather as an imperative that was not only inappropriate coming from strangers but intrusive and unrealistic. She knew, of course, that the people who said such things were only trying to ingratiate themselves with her and cast the inevitable cloak of informality over everything. No one cared what kind of day she would have. She preferred formality. Though it was an overreaction, she always had to fight the impulse to say, "I'm going through a divorce right now so my days aren't very pleasant, but thanks."

In Colorado, "Have a good day" had become "Have a good one," and this vagueness was comforting to Sylvia. Even in her present state of mind, she could imagine having a good *something*, as long as it didn't have to be a complete day. But a great day was too much. She was of half a mind to call the case manager back but she settled the receiver in its cradle instead. For some reason she thought of her father, a bald gruff man with a red face and a brusque manner. When he had last visited, a clerk in the video store had instructed him to have a nice night as he was leaving. Sylvia's father turned to the boy and said, "I'm seventy-two years old. My night is over."

She had seen Charlie Steinmetz twice since her separation, once for coffee and another time they had taken a walk in Washington Park and watched the swans and children. She wasn't ready to bring him home yet, but exposure hadn't lessened her interest in him. It was nice to be around a man again; the simple truth was that she had never thought of her husband as being a man. It wasn't what she had valued in him, when she had valued him. He was more of a maid, or perhaps a wife. It seemed disloyal, but she didn't have pleasant memories of Mitchell though they hadn't fought or been unkind to one another. Maybe that was the problem, a complete lack of passion of any sort.

Charlie was completely different. He was compact, solid, with muscular arms and a handsome face that would unexpectedly break up into the most beautiful smile she had ever seen. Yet it went beyond his features, which were pleasant enough; when Charlie Steinmetz smiled, you felt as if you were the most privileged person in the world.

Now they were meeting for dinner and though it wasn't a nice restaurant and therefore not terribly serious, as Sylvia waited, she had for the first time in years a romantic image of herself. She imagined someone else, someone she didn't know, observing her alone at the corner table, or perhaps seeing her through the window from the street, and thinking that she looked wistful, or, no, not wistful but thoughtful, and something else beside that. Not lonely exactly; alone, but content to be so, on the cusp of something meaningful. Thinking of herself in this way made her smile from embarrassment. She spilled a few drops of water on the table and was drawing in the droplets when Charlie approached.

"Sorry I'm late," he said, a note of anxiety in his voice.

He was wearing a blue blazer over a knit shirt. Sylvia thought worry actually improved his looks. "You're not," she said. "I was early for a change."

Charlie ran his fingers through his hair and grimaced. "I was just talking to my lawyer," he said. "Scary. I don't think I ever had a lawyer before."

Sylvia liked the fact that he just jumped into things without pleasantries or meaningless inquiries about her day. This was what mattered, let's get into it, he seemed to say, communicating an intimacy she liked. After all, their marriages and divorce were in a way the only subjects between them: were they free? "What did he say?"

Charlie shrugged. "You know, to him it's a case. I mean, I think he's a good guy and he's interested, sort of. But when his assistant asked if it was going to be complicated, the divorce, I mean, he shook his head and told her she could leave. You know, no problem. I can handle this. He might just have been trying to save me money on the paralegal, but to me, it's pretty complicated, I can tell you that."

Sylvia nodded in what she hoped was a sympathetic way. But what Charlie said about the lawyer made her think of her own practice, of all the patients with their illnesses and injuries, real and imagined and whether she cared enough. They were all cases to her, they had to be. If she were emotionally involved with the patients who came to her for help she'd be useless, torn up by the tragedy of the quotidian. For it was all tragic, she thought, and rather than being dramatic tragedy turned out to be ordinary, routine, the kind of thing that happened when you weren't paying attention and then came to dominate your life. Doctors were trained to ignore this in medical school, to push it out of their minds. That's why law and medicine were called professions, teaching, too. Charlie might not put it this way but Sylvia thought his students were probably also cases to him, names in a grade book, forgotten as soon as the last exam was completed. All of them, doctors, lawyers, professors were paid friends and confidants, but Sylvia saw nothing wrong with that. She covered his hand with hers. "Getting divorced is hard," she said. "I hate it."

Charlie smiled and the attractive bleakness was replaced by a sudden warm interest in her." Me, too," he said. "The only thing worse would be to go on being married to these people, right?" Without waiting for her answer, he grabbed the menu. "What do you want to eat?" he asked. "I'm starving."

To Sylvia's surprise, her first patient when she was back in the clinic was Tom Chapin. He looked much the same: high white forehead, lips stretched tight across his teeth in what Sylvia guessed was supposed to be a smile. She leaned back in her chair and pulled her lab coat tight to her chest. "I didn't expect to see you again, Mr. Chapin," she said. "Patients who complain to their insurance companies don't usually come back."

Chapin ducked his head and Sylvia realized the man was embarrassed. "I didn't want you thinking I was a drug addict," he said. "It bothered me that you didn't believe me, bothered me to have to ask for those damned pills." Tears started in his brown eyes and he brushed them away with an angry sweep of his hand.

Sylvia waited a moment. It touched her that her opinion was important to him. She said, "It wasn't that I didn't believe you, Mr. Chapin; it was that I didn't know you, that you weren't my patient. I only prescribe for people I know, patients I've examined before. But pain is nothing to be embarrassed about."

Chapin nodded, his large head looking like an under-ripe melon in the florescent light of the office. "Well, I'm your patient now," he said. "I asked for you at the desk and they said okay." He slid his forms across the desk as if to convince her.

Sylvia had to repress a smile at the irony of the situation, but she knew she should be used to the unexpected or unlikely by now. After all, Mrs. Mankwitz had said she was the only doctor her husband wanted to see and he'd tried to get her license taken away. She smiled and wrote "Idiopathic back pain" in the space reserved for her diagnosis and got to her feet.

Chapin squinted at the paper and asked, "What's that, what I got?"

Sylvia shrugged. "It's not what you have. I don't know what you have, except I know you have pain. What I wrote just means there's no obvious cause for it, like an illness or an injury at work."

Chapin nodded his head slowly, taking it in. "But you believe me when I say it's there, the pain?" This seemed to be the thing that interested him most.

"Oh, yes," Sylvia said. "I even think there's a reason. There's a reason for everything. We just don't know what it is yet."

This seemed to surprise Chapin. "You're going to find it, though, right?"

"I don't know," Sylvia said. "That's the hardest thing about being a doctor and the most frustrating thing for patients. I'm going to try, that's all I can say. Now, I'd like you to lie down on the table so I can examine you."

"I've already been examined," Chapin protested. "It's all there," he said, pointing at the thick case file on her desk.

Sylvia patted the big man on the shoulder. "I know that, Mr. Chapin. But I haven't examined you and since no one found anything before, we're just going to start all over again."

Chapin looked at her, resigned and rose to his feet. "Okay, you're the boss."

In that moment, Sylvia realized that this was the problem; that she had never felt like the boss, not just in the office but in her life, never felt in control, and it seemed that now perhaps finally after everything that was what she was coming to, and the elusive search for first causes might be over. The idiopathic pain of living would be with her forever, but she would learn to manage and even control it, just as her patient would have to live with his.

She felt her anger and frustration with the slow pace of the divorce, with Mitchell and the limitations of life in general fade in favor of a lighter feeling that she might have called optimism had she ever experienced it before. But now she had to focus on the patient in front of her and decide whether there was any serious cause for what he was feeling or if pain was simply something he would have to put up with for the duration. She put her hands together in front of her and said, "You're right about that, Mr. Chapin. But in order for me to be a good boss, I need you up on the table."

Now Chapin smiled and got on the table. "Well, all right then," he said. "Let's go."

CHAPTER NINE

Given Sylvia's threat not to return after the last mediation session, Mitchell had suggested they try something new. Sylvia was tired of it all but felt guilty about pulling the plug altogether which is why they were in a psychologist's office in what was often called "couch canyon" in Denver. It was mid-winter, gray and foreboding with a dirty scrim of snow in the streets. It wasn't one of Denver's 300 hundred sunny days in the year and a storm was coming in. When Sylvia lived in Chicago they called February the suicide season. Denver wasn't that bad, but Sylvia wasn't feeling hopeful.

"I have to say this feels a lot like couples therapy," she told an earnest young social worker named Tony who'd been assigned to them. "I don't mean to be harsh but I really don't think we ought to be here. I know I want a divorce and, whatever he says, I think Mitchell does too. That's why we were in mediation, to try to work out all the details. This feels like a step backwards to me." She gestured at some brightly colored charts on the table in front of them.

"I understand that you feel that way," Tony said, "but we find that couples work better after a divorce if the process is more pleasant, orderly."

Sylvia didn't want to risk looking like even more of a bitch than she already did so instead of asking who "we" was exactly, she sat back in her chair, resigned. "Okay, what do you want us to do?"

Tony smiled again. This was one of his good qualities and it was clear that he knew it. "I want each of you to fill out this questionnaire and then we can look at your responses and maybe come up with some conclusions about where to go next."

This sounded like it could take a while and Sylvia had a full morning of appointments. "Fine," she said. "But I'll have to take mine with me and get it back to you." She picked up the questionnaire and read: "Are You Co-Dependent?" She raised her eyebrows at Tony. "You're serious about this?"

"It's actually a pretty good instrument," Tony replied. "We've had a lot of success with it."

"Okay," Sylvia said and walked out of the room, leaving Mitchell and Tony looking at each other.

"I don't have any more appointments today," Mitchell said. "I think I'll just stay and do the questionnaire."

"It shouldn't take more than a half an hour," Tony said. "Just read the statements and write down your reactions." Then he left the room.

Mitchell opened the booklet and sat down to confront his future. A series of highlighted phrases were printed on the pages with spaces left open, presumably for the subjects to write their responses. Mitchell didn't feel like writing anything but he was the one who'd suggested they see the social worker.

My good feelings about who I am stem from being liked by you.
It would have been good if feelings were all that were involved in his marriage, Mitchell thought, but it went beyond that. All of his

ideas, at least all the ones he could remember, stemmed from his relationship with Sylvia, so that when they stopped having a relationship, which was where he guessed they were now, he hardly knew who he was at all. He didn't know what foods he liked, what films he preferred, or what kinds of clothes he would have picked if he picked out his own clothes, had she not told him, which, inevitably, she did, or had. So that while what he had won by moving out was a kind of liberation, it placed him in a state of virtual paralysis in other ways. It wasn't really as bad as this sounded, but "stemmed?" The statement suggested that feelings were like fragile roots growing from a submerged seed. He thought he must have had feelings before meeting her, even if he couldn't remember much about what they were, but they had been together a long time, they had children together. Still, "good feelings?" He wasn't sure, just as he didn't know if he had actually been liked by her. If so, he hadn't been conscious of it for a while. They'd loved each other once, he was sure of that. But when love was gone separation seemed like a natural thing to do. Yet he regretted it, not the separation but the loss of what they'd had: a family. He had always liked to walk into the kids' bedrooms at night and watch them sleep. He could still do that on the weekend when they stayed in his small apartment, but it wasn't the same.

My mental attention is focused on manipulating you to do it my way.

Sylvia read the statement, then re-read it. She wondered if Mitchell had actually written these things himself or if there were some kind of cosmic joke being played on her. His way, her way, the truth was Mitchell had never been skilled enough to manipulate anyone or anything, so it seemed to fall to her to take charge. But was that manipulation or simply taking control when it was necessary? She could see that manipulation might be a goal for some people; the idea that life was pliable, plastic, manageable and therefore could be arranged in a way that made sense, but she'd never gotten there. But of course the word had other connotations, suggesting she might be some kind of clever machiavel intent on bending others to her will through subtle means. She seldom felt this powerful. The image in her mind was of a person pushing a barge through a swamp, sweeping reeds out of the way as she made slow progress, dodging alligators. In this paradigm would she be manipulating the barge? Even this much control seemed enviable to Sylvia.

My self esteem is bolstered by relieving your pain.
There was that pain thing again. Mitchell wondered if he was reacting properly to this but Tony had said there were no right or wrong answers. Still, he felt the statements implied judgments of him and his life, seeming to suggest one either had too much or too little pain, and thus an excess or too little self esteem. He had never thought about this but even if it was true, he didn't see what either pain or self esteem had to with the present situation. He knew he had never thought of improving his self esteem by relieving Sylvia's pain, that much was certain. He'd tried to make things easier for her, that was true, by taking care of the children, doing some cooking, cleaning up the house, simple tasks that needed doing. But no one would call these necessary chores painful. Maybe what they meant by self esteem was the absence of pain but the nights when she'd left the room in tears or screamed at him in frustration seemed to speak of some kind of pain she'd suffered, at least in the last days of their life together. And whether or not he'd borne the responsibility she'd assigned him for that, he knew relieving it hadn't bolstered his self esteem. The statement made no sense.

My hobbies and interests are put aside. My time is spent sharing your interests and hobbies.
Who had interests or hobbies? Sylvia wondered. In the abstract, sure; if someone were to ask her, say, on a job application, she could

come up with something. She played the piano, or she used to; she liked to read fiction and even wrote a little herself; she still went to yoga classes when she had time. But no one she knew, at least no one with kids, had real hobbies, except Mitchell with his stamp collecting. But that was all. None of their friends belonged to clubs where the members wore blazers with crests and funny hats or got together at regular intervals. People she knew *did* things, often with a mad passion, like skiing or running or climbing. This was Colorado, after all. Sylvia had never enjoyed winter sports and only participated in them occasionally out of guilt. She felt obliged to be active, no matter how she happened to be feeling. Hobbies were different. She thought of Ozzie Nelson in the cardigan looking up with a smile from a hot game of checkers with Harriet in the old TV show. She tried to think. She used to sew but at this remove she didn't even know where her sewing machine was. They had gone to the movies and to restaurants before the kids came, but were those really hobbies? The more she thought about the questionnaire the more she believed that during their marriage she and Mitchell had occupied parallel universes, oddly lacking things others seemed to take for granted. Maybe that was the point of the exercise.

Your clothing and personal appearance are dictated by my desires as I feel you are a reflection of me.

Mitchell liked the way his wife looked, the way she dressed and carried herself and he always had. And not just her clothes, but her long legs, shiny black hair and what he thought of as her aristocratic bearing. Still, he had never thought he had the slightest effect on her in this regard. She might ask him about her hair or a dress and in the beginning he might have offered an opinion, and then she might even have listened. Usually, however, she seemed to do the opposite of what he had suggested. If he expressed a preference for pastels, she'd choose bold colors; if he said he preferred her hair long, she'd have it cut in a bob; if he said he liked flats, she'd buy expensive heels. Once he protested, saying she paid no attention to him so why ask what he thought, but she said she was interested, even if she wasn't persuaded that he was right. This seemed to take care of it until she had stopped asking, assuming, he guessed, that they would only disagree, as they did about so many other things. She took to wearing capes, dark with daring satin linings and sometimes, a beret or babushka. There were some purple boots and bright scarves. He had wondered if perhaps she was dressing for some else. The suggestion now, on this form, that his opinion of her clothes would actually matter, that she would dress to please him, was almost intoxicating. It was as if this room, with its violet pillows and throws had suddenly been drenched in musk. He let his mind roam over the statement. What if he did actually have the influence they suggested? He would ask her to wear lots of fuchsia and lace, maybe diaphanous underwear or a black garter belt, though he didn't know about that. Opaque stockings and perhaps backless heels, the shoes they called "fuck-me-nows" in Los Angeles. As he developed his fantasy, however, he realized that what he was thinking about was how to make her look sexy, which would have meant that desire would again be part of their lives, and this made him sad. She had never been his reflection; he wasn't sure there was anything much to reflect. He avoided mirrors, reflecting pools at fountains, even shiny surfaces and car windows. He wasn't much to look at but what he was most afraid of was seeing nothing. It had been a long time for them to come to this. But that had nothing to do with clothes, or with his desires.

My fear of your anger determines what I say or do.
To Sylvia, this was the most ludicrous prompt so far. She not only wasn't afraid of Mitchell's anger, she would have welcomed it, as she would any show of emotion, any excessive loss of control, anything that he might have considered untoward. That could have saved them, Sylvia thought. And because Mitchell never expressed the

anger she thought he must feel, she often felt out of control, embarrassed by her own anger at him, even when she thought it was perfectly understandable and deserved. She was the bitch; he was the nice guy, ever patient, always waiting for her to regain herself. She hated that and hated it in them. She wanted to say, to plead with Mitchell, to just lose it in some extraordinary, even unfair way, but he never would. Fear of his anger? Not in this lifetime, alas.

My social circle diminishes as I involve myself with you.
The questions reminded Mitchell of a Yugoslavian phrase book he'd once bought for a trip to Eastern Europe. Where can I have my suit pressed? Where can I buy a corsage for my wife? Does the hotel have a shoeshine stand? Mitchell had neither a suit nor shoes that needed shining but he had felt oddly guilty for having none of the proscribed needs listed in the book. It was kind of like the hobbies question. The stated expectation of manners and institutions in the world made him painfully aware of his own failures. After all, why didn't he have a suit or shoes suitable for shining? Why didn't he buy his wife flowers more often? As for "social circles," they had none. Occasionally she would remark on this in an accusatory way, as if he should somehow go out and discover a group of fun people to invite over for fondue and Trivial Pursuit. He guessed they could learn how to play bridge and then join a group, but he wasn't sure she'd go for this. He gathered from television and the movies that other people did belong to such groups, that often they got together with people they had known since college and with whom they were intimate. The men went to ball games together and the women shopped and played cards. Sometimes, Mitchell guessed, the whole entourage would go on trips and later complain jokingly about one or another of the couples not having been adventurous enough. Then they would gather to make wonderful dinners with home-made pasta in large kitchens with wood floors and bright tiled countertops. Afterwards, they would

show slides from a trip. They would laugh uproariously at jokes only they understood. Feelings would be hurt, someone would feel slighted and then they'd make up, never having actually fought and all would be well. At the end, they'd agree that they needed to do this more often. His life with Sylvia was nothing like this. He couldn't remember when they'd had anyone over for dinner or been invited out. Their colleges were far away and they lived in a city that was foreign to both of them, a city with too many cars and not enough sidewalks. They went to work and then came home where they sat in glum silence trying desperately to think of something to say. Or at least he did. At work a young woman had sought him out. She stopped by his office several times to ask inconsequential questions and finally mentioned that when she was a graduate student she had once sat in the audience when he delivered a lecture at the business school she attended. What he said then determined her choice of career. It was both flattering and depressing since he could only barely remember the lecture or what he had said there. The young woman pursued him, however. She asked him to lunch, and, in time, let him know she was available should he be interested. He found this so surprising that he couldn't even think whether or not she appealed to him. After he moved out into the apartment, he decided he was actually interested, though he hadn't told the young woman yet.

I put my values aside in order to connect with you.
Sylvia sat back and looked out her window at the gathering darkness. She actually liked being shut in this way, closed off from the world and other people by weather, even if in Colorado it was always transient. She looked back at the booklet. She wondered what values they were talking about exactly. Maybe it wasn't Tony at all, but some Christian Right/Family Values groups that put this together? In the welter of psychobabble it was sometimes hard to tell. She tried to think seriously about values. She wouldn't

murder anyone or rob a bank, but she might stretch the truth with Mitchell, in fact she knew she did. What did they mean by connecting? She remembered reading E.M. Forster in college. "Only connect." She knew this had nothing to do with the questionnaire but she liked the idea of social workers reading *Howards End* and the memory of her English professor, tall and melancholy in gray tweed reading aloud to the class. In this case "connect" seemed to connote a bargain, *quid pro quo*: you do this for me and I'll do that for you. Vulgarizing a fairly lofty idea. She thought about what really mattered to her in life, the idea that things *did* matter and weren't just part of a random loblolly spilling out without rhyme or reason. Loyalty would certainly be there for her, and yet she was divorcing her husband and thinking of starting up a relationship with another man. She tried to put this out of her mind. It wasn't really what they were asking, she thought. Besides Tony had said to just answer the questions without thinking about them too much, a hard assignment for Sylvia, not thinking. She sat for a moment, paralyzed by some half-understood profundity. Then she realized she was thinking again. Maybe that was it: her real problem was thinking. She should just act, or perhaps, connect.

I value your opinion and way of doing things more than my own. There it was again, like an unbidden telemarketer, values. His, hers, and who set whose aside for whom? Mitchell was beginning to think that his problem was that he didn't value things enough because, truthfully, he seldom thought about it, what he valued. He stumbled from place to place, job to job, situation to situation, doing the best he could, and usually doing whatever was just good enough. But he was always flying by the seat of his pants. He knew this and sometimes felt guilty about it. Did others weigh every decision carefully and only then do whatever needed to be done because they valued one thing over another? His life seemed more random than that, more purposeless, though not less important, at least to him. He tried to think of a specific situation that might reflect his values, like moving from one place to another, or having children. He knew people who rationalized their decisions earnestly, saying they couldn't imagine bringing children into a corrupt world, for example. He noticed that in these cases idealism did not often induce people to give their money to African charities, however, nor did it prevent them from buying expensive cars or second homes. In his life with Sylvia, Mitchell knew they had used her system, mostly because she had one. It worked reasonably well and he found he had few regrets about the decisions that they had made, so he supposed he valued her way of doing things more than he did his own. Indeed the only independent decision he could remember making was when he met his wife. He had fallen immediately, achingly in love and pursued her with an urgency that surprised him. She had protested that she was just coming off a failed engagement and wasn't ready for a new relationship, but he didn't care and in the end he won out. Since then, however, he had been glad to give over his opinions, such as they were, his values, and whatever else was necessary in order to be with her. When had all that changed, he wondered.

The quality of my life is in relation to the quality of yours.
Sylvia focused on the language and wondered if this was a defense, a way of not thinking deeply about things, just as skepticism was. All the questions seemed to be about good feelings or values or connections or self-esteem or, now, quality of life. She questioned the assumptions. What if one lived life without expecting it to be good or connected or full of value? Was this possible in the world of the survey? It wasn't a question of whether this was good or bad; bad was a quality just as good was and something that couldn't be quantified. What mattered were one's expectations, which in turn led to feelings of rejection or discouragement. She hadn't expected much from Mitchell when she had married him but at some

point that stopped working, the lack of expectations. She thought he was actually a good man and a good father. There was nothing wrong with him from an objective point of view. She just didn't want to be married to him anymore. Nevertheless after reading the questions she realized that until now the quality of her life had definitely been in relation to the quality of his; this seemed obvious. If she was unhappy, then her quality of life could hardly be called wonderful and no doubt the same was true of Mitchell. The survey seemed to imply that we should all live life independently of others, even those we're married to, and that just seemed wrong. She thought again about quality of life, the idea that it had quality or could have it. In her own way, Sylvia thought this was really what the divorce was all about: dissatisfaction with life as she lived it and the hope that things could improve. For the first time since she'd started filling out the questions, she felt optimistic.

She thought of the social worker's office, color-coordinated in warm peach, mauve, dusty rose, with bright pillows everywhere. It was supposed to make you feel peaceful, she thought. She wondered if there was an observation window on one of the walls, a hidden eye concealed behind the bucolic Homers depicting boys at play in a freshly-mown field. She hadn't really answered most of the questions, but she'd go back and return the survey anyway because she'd promised to do so. In the end, she thought the questions were useful. They'd made her think, but she had to get back to Tony's office right away because her time was up.

CHAPTER TEN

Sylvia felt as if she were slogging through a swamp, her legs aching, her vision blurred. For the past week, she had had dreams in which she was bound and gagged or strapped in a strait jacket. The constant was the feeling of a lack of mobility, something that was not entirely mysterious given that she was a neurologist with many patients who felt this way every day of their waking lives. Now she shook her head and forced herself to focus. "I'm sorry, Mr. Whitley," she said. "I didn't hear all of what you were just saying."

He was a tall thin man in his fifties who had come to her a week before complaining of leg problems, numbness below the knee. Yet he was having no difficulty with his balance and Sylvia had tested his reflexes and gone over his legs with a pin. His reflexes were brisk and he reported no consistent loss of sensation in the affected area. She could see nothing that was obviously wrong and she wasn't even sure why his primary care physician had referred him to a specialist. Maybe she was missing something or it may have been that the other doctor just wanted to turf a demanding patient who had been making his life difficult. It wouldn't have been the first time.

"It's that," Whitley said now, pointing at an area six inches above his ankle.

Sylvia nodded. She saw nothing. "What, exactly?" she asked.

Whitley sighed in exasperation. "That," he said, punching his leg. "It's swollen. You *can* see that, can't you?"

The leg did appear to be slightly swollen, but when Sylvia palpated the area she felt no mass and it wasn't discolored. "Does that hurt?" she asked.

"No," Whitley said, not happy but somewhat mollified that Sylvia had at least validated his vision. "Is it cancer?"

Sylvia checked the impulse to laugh. Self-diagnosis was a major cause of patient visits. People would see something on the "Today" show or read a newspaper health column and come in certain that they were suffering from the same disease as some celebrity. It was an enormous waste of time, but in the age of managed care it would be useless to counsel patients to simply trust in the diagnostic skills of their doctors. Every home library now included a *Physicians' Desk Reference* and chat sites on the internet were available for every conceivable malady. "I'm quite certain it's not cancer," she said.

"Then what is it?" Whitley asked.

Sylvia took a deep breath and leaned against the wall. Simon had been up in the middle of the night crying and when she had gone to him, he said, "Leave me alone. I want my dad." Sylvia had sat on the edge of the boy's bed for an hour while he excoriated her for driving Mitchell away. She had learned it did little good to try to explain things to an eight-year-old, so she just listened and finally he let her hold him and then he went to sleep.

"Let me make sure I understand everything you've told me so far, Mr. Whitley," she said in what she hoped was a patient tone of voice. She re-checked her notes. "You say this lump appeared four or five months ago, or at least you first noticed it then, but there's no pain, no sustained unsteadiness, and except for a kind of undifferentiated numbness that comes and goes, no symptomatic distress." She hesitated. Then she said, "And last month you ran in The New York City Marathon. Is all this correct?"

The man nodded. There were white spots on either side of his pinched nostrils as if he were going to cry. He shook his head and looked angrily at Sylvia. "What's wrong with me," he asked again. "I know this isn't normal, so why won't any of you people tell me what's wrong?"

Sylvia leaned forward and looked into her patient's eyes, trying not to sound exasperated because she understood, or thought she did. It was awful to be convinced that something was wrong without being able to find out what it was. "I'm sorry to have to tell you this, Mr. Whitley, because obviously this has taken up a lot of your time and emotional energy, but as far as I can tell, there's nothing wrong with you." She snapped the folder shut and patted him on the arm. "If anything changes, though, I want you to call me. Have a nice day."

In her office, she checked her voice mail for messages but her mind was still in the examining room. She knew she had been dismissive and she regretted it. She hated to lose her temper, and she hadn't really, but what was done was done. It wasn't that Mr. Whitley was unusual, though it wasn't often that she saw marathoners. Most of her patients were fortunate if they could walk without the aid of a cane. But any doctor who was honest would admit that three-quarters of the patients she saw were either beyond help or had nothing wrong with them. The art of medicine lay in being able to accurately diagnose and treat the remaining twenty-five per cent, which was where Sylvia tried to put her energy. But that wasn't Mr. Whitley's fault. First feed the face, then talk about right and wrong, she told herself. Even when it was difficult, her responsibility was not only to show compassion for her patients but to feel it. Whitley had been scared and sought help, which was entirely appropriate. It wasn't even very different from what she had been feeling lately, though she hadn't consulted her doctor. She *was* the doctor, for God's sake.

Sylvia had noticed that when she and Gregory met it was either in *faux* gourmet restaurants or over-priced places where the captains addressed him as professor. Neither she nor Gregory cared much about food and she had never thought of him as being particularly arrogant or concerned about titles. She supposed the restaurants he chose had something to do with keeping up appearances, which seemed to have become increasingly important as he'd got older.

She thought of the first time they met. Mitchell had brought her home on a college vacation from Chicago and she'd been nervous about meeting her future father-in-law, whom even her college pathology professor had revered. She needn't have been anxious. Small and lively, with quick gray eyes, Gregory made clear his interest in Sylvia from the start, interviewing her about her family, the courses she was taking and her outside interests while his wife and son sat politely listening. Before the evening was out, Gregory confided that she was the best thing ever to happen to Mitchell, while implying that there had not been much competition in this regard. When Sylvia protested that they'd just met, Gregory looked into her eyes and told her he had great faith in first impressions.

As taken as she was with Gregory's manners and self-confidence, however, Sylvia knew that in part it was everything else about the family that drew her to Mitchell, everything, that is, that was different from her own family. The slightly shabby but valuable Mission furniture, the original oil paintings by family friends, the dog-eared collections of poetry that someone had actually read, the pictures of forgotten relatives wearing blazers and white ducks at lawn parties, the ancient Volvo with the dragging tail pipe. Everything that said 'We don't care what others think; we set our own standards here.' Sylvia had never been directly exposed to this kind of quiet self-assurance, even if she knew it was largely possible because of the family inheritance that made such things as job security irrelevant.

Sylvia had understood from the start that Mitchell was a disappointment to his father, though Gregory would not have been an easy father for any son to satisfy and it seemed unfair that Mitchell should even have to measure up. She also realized that since Gregory didn't take pride in his son, the pretty young woman whom Mitchell had inexplicably persuaded to accompany him home provided an excellent alternative. Which is to say that the romance, if there was one, was always between Gregory and Sylvia with Mitchell the odd man out. When they married, Sylvia felt it was an effort on Mitchell's part to legitimize himself in his father's eyes. Yet when she had asked Gregory after the ceremony if she could call him father, he said simply, "I'm not actually your father, am I?" Sylvia felt too hurt to respond or even speak of it again and it was only much later that she understood the reason was that Gregory always thought of her more as his lover than as a daughter or even a daughter-in-law.

Now Gregory appeared at her side. "Sorry I'm late," he said. She smiled. He was always late and she always forgave him.

"It's okay," she said. "It gave me time to think about a case I had this morning."

"Anything interesting?" Gregory said lightly. He had given up private practice he once told her because he got tired of looking at runny noses and sore throats all day.

"Not really," Sylvia said. "Just troubling."

Gregory nodded. He made a show of looking at the menu though he always ordered the same thing: ginger ale, lime lettuce salad and coffee. Now he looked at her. "So, you've actually done it," he said.

Sylvia knew what he meant. "Not completely," she said. "But yes, we're getting divorced."

Gregory bowed his head and looked at the table as if he was the one who'd been left. When Sylvia and Mitchell had separated before, she was still in the residency and on the verge of becoming involved with another doctor. Gregory brought them together in his living room and said sternly, "Do you realize how many people you'd be letting down if you divorced? Do you understand how selfish you're being?"

This time, however, he seemed reserved, even accepting. It was if he'd become too old and tired to object. "Well, you're adults," Gregory said at last. "You have to live your own lives, I guess."

Sylvia nodded and took his hand. "My life will always include you, you know."

Generally, such expressions embarrassed Gregory and caused him to back away but this time was different. He looked at her and there was water in his eyes. "I know," he said. "Thank god for that at least."

At the hospital, Sylvia sleepwalked through her rounds and then went to the cafeteria for coffee. She was sitting alone in something approaching a fugue state when she heard a familiar voice. "May I interrupt your thoughts?" Cory Weintraub asked.

Cory was an old friend from medical school. They had shared night call as residents and often occupied the small bunk beds where medical students tried to catch a few hours of sleep during slack times in the ED. "Piss poor sleep," Cory had called it then, and she agreed, though what was in a sense more interesting was that he never made a pass at her during those lost nights. Internship was an intense experience and those who shared it often became romantically involved, sometimes with disastrous results.

Now Sylvia found she was pleased to see Cory. He had the same steel-wool hair, if a bit grayer, and had put on a few pounds. These days, however, on the few occasions when they ran into each other, rather than complaining about sleep deprivation, Cory usually went on about his cash-flow problems. To hear him tell it, he was on the edge of destitution, but the truth was he had married a woman from a wealthy eastern family and her expectations had become his. A second home in the mountains and summer vacations in Nantucket would take a serious bite out of anyone's salary. "You're not interrupting anything," Sylvia said. "Have a chair."

Cory set down his tray and started spooning yogurt into his mouth with the practiced grace of a man accustomed to brief lunch breaks. "The word on the street is you and Mitch are getting divorced," he said. He looked at her and raised his eyebrows. "Correct or incorrect? Not that you have to tell me."

Sylvia indicated that this time at least the gossip was accurate and Cory nodded in what she supposed was sympathy.

"I'm sorry, but not that sorry," he said. "That guy was never right for you." Cory shook his head in mock despair. "Anyway, typical of my luck. Here I am married and in important debt when the girl of my dreams becomes available. Why couldn't you have done this five years ago?" He winked to let her know he was neither entirely serious nor only joking.

It cheered Sylvia to have a man flirt with her, even someone who would never have interested her. She wasn't sure how many men would take a chance on a thirty-five year old woman with two young children. "I probably should have," Sylvia said. "Maybe ten years ago. Maybe never have started in the first place. I guess I thought I should get married, that that's what women did, even women who were doctors. God knows why we stayed together this long. I don't think either of us was very happy. Inertia, I guess. What I can't figure out, though, is why I feel this way."

"What way?" Cory asked. He had moved without hesitation from the yogurt to a green salad. "Don't worry," he said, as if she had been put off by his table manners. "I'm listening. It's what I do."

"Since I got what I wanted," Sylvia said, almost to herself, "why aren't I satisfied, even happy? It's the damndest thing. I mean, I'm a zombie, and I can't afford that. My patients are really sick; they need me to be paying attention to what they're saying. I don't have to tell you; you know what a neurology practice is like." She hesitated, then plunged on again. "And it's not that I don't try, but sometimes I'm pinching myself underneath the examining table just to stay awake. Last month I was getting sued by a guy who thought he was in direct contact with god and when we persuaded him to drop the suit he started calling my home, just to talk, he said, and as weird as it was, it hardly dented my consciousness. You know, my kids would call me to the phone, "Mom, it's that Moses guy again," and it would mean nothing to me. Well, not nothing, but not as much as it should have meant. It's funny but not that funny. I have no appetite, and when I'm able to sleep I'm having some unbelievable dreams. Does that make any kind of sense to you?"

Cory paused, spoon poised above a bowl of pudding. He looked at her. "Is that a professional question?" he asked.

"Sure," Sylvia said, not knowing when she had started getting serious. "I guess so. What's the point of having friends who are psychiatrists otherwise?"

Cory nodded. "I just want to know if I can deduct the lunch," he said. Then he patted her hand. "Sorry, I don't mean to be a wise guy. Really. Look, I've got a patient at two, which gives us fifteen minutes to sort this out. Why don't you come down to my office?"

It always depressed Sylvia to see how much better other physicians kept their offices than she did. Often there would be original art or mementos from trips to exotic places and, of course, diplomas and honorary degrees. Cory's office was small but cozy, with a leather couch, matching wing chair, and a wall of books framing a computer stand. Although Sylvia had hired a decorator when she moved in, now her desk was piled high with files and dying plants and the furniture seemed less planned than a collection of occasional enthusiasms eventually cast aside. Besides feeling inadequate about it, however, she hadn't really done anything. One weekend when she had managed to find time to come in and clean up, a patient asked if she was moving. It was, she thought, symptomatic of the general disorganization of her life.

They sat across from each other and Cory said, "Tell me what's going on. Don't worry about making sense. Just say whatever comes to mind. Words and phrases. What's wrong with your life?"

"I don't really know," Sylvia said. "Nothing, I guess. Everything. I just feel exhausted and overwhelmed all the time and kind of bleak. Which is odd because I was the one who wanted the divorce; I was incredibly relieved when Mitchell finally moved out. I couldn't stand to look at that man anymore. Couldn't stand his goddamned hair plugs, his phony voice, that fake English smoking jacket he insisted on wearing, his forgetfulness which he thinks is intellectual." She shivered involuntarily. "It's unfair, I know but I couldn't stand anything about him. Not to mention sharing the same bed. So why aren't I jumping for joy? Why do I feel tragic all the time?"

Cory shrugged. "Typical doctor. You want to prescribe your own feelings. All of that happened so you *should* feel this way or that."

Sylvia smiled. "I guess so. What did they say on the surgery rotation: if there's a problem, fix the problem; no problem."

"Right," Cory said. "Except there is a problem, because no matter what kind of a *schlemiel* Mitch is, he's been your *schlemiel* for, what, ten years?"

Sylvia nodded. "Twelve, but close enough. It seems longer."

Cory smiled, his forehead wrinkling in a reassuring way. "A relationship is like a habit. There are good habits and bad habits, but they're all hard to break, even if it's the best thing for you. What you're feeling is what shrinks call Uncomplicated Bereavement. You could look it up," he said, pointing at the bookshelf. "It's in the DSM-V. Pretty natural for people with any kind of a loss. A death in the family. Serious illness."

"You'd call divorce a loss?" Sylvia asked.

Cory looked as if he was going to laugh. "Are you kidding? Of course it's a loss. Big time. Marriage is an incredibly idealistic institution. You meet this person and you're what, twenty-five? You fall in love and then you're supposed to live the rest of your lives together. Wild. And if by some accident this actually happens, it's not considered unusual but the norm." He settled in his chair, warming to the topic. "Think about it, marriage is about the only life choice you make at that age. You don't decide where you're going to live, what job you're going to have, what kind of car you're going to drive, how you're going to dress. You don't decide anything important about your life when you're in your twenties, except who you're going to be with until you die. That's all."

Sylvia laughed. "I have to say I never thought of it that way."

Cory nodded. "No one does, trust me. Anyway, giving up that image of yourself as a married couple is a major blow to the ego. Put that together with the propaganda you're fed in medical school about being super-human and you come to accept the idea that you can accomplish anything, even something as unrealistic as marriage. Crazy, but it's true. And the rest of society conspires in this by treating you as if you're contagious if you decide to break up. A whole industry has developed just to help people get divorced. I get their propaganda all the time."

"Exactly. I get attacked in the JCC parking lot when I go to pick my kids up. I'm a home-wrecker, even if it's my own home I wrecked. It's not like we had a lot of friends before, but they all seem to be siding with Mitchell. As if it wasn't enough, I'm bucking the Denver Jewish establishment."

Cory smiled. "There is one? An establishment in Denver?" He came from Chicago and looked as Denver as little more than a cow town.

"Believe it or not," Sylvia said. "And they take themselves very seriously."

Cory nodded as if this made sense then he glanced at the clock and launched into his conclusion. "You're well rid of him if you ask me, and the good news is that now you're part of a sub-culture and depending on your age, sex, and religion, and whether or not kids are involved, there's a group right for you somewhere. There are lunch groups, singles clubs at temples and churches. Not a joiner? It's okay, there are books, newspaper, articles, interactive videos, take your pick. After all that, if you're lucky, you'll meet someone else, maybe at a group, maybe somewhere else, and start all over again." He hesitated and looked up at her with a smile. "Am I even close to what you're going through?"

"Close enough," Sylvia said. Cory made divorce sound not only reasonable but inevitable. But she still couldn't get used to the idea that her condition was described in the most recent edition of the Diagnostic and Statistical Manual, the bible of psychiatrists. Unless they could cite a diagnosis from the DSM-V, insurance companies would never authorize psychiatric treatment or drugs, much less hospitalization of their patients, no matter how sick they were. "Leave it to doctors to imagine that grief could ever be uncompli-cated," Sylvia said.

"If it goes on for more than six months, it becomes compli-cated," Cory said and smiled to show he wasn't serious. "It doesn't mean you don't feel bad; it just means it's natural given the situa-tion. And I'm sorry, but that's all the time we have today." He rose and put his arms around Sylvia. She found it comforting to hug the small man, even while she wondered if he had subtly proposi-tioned her. Cory held her at arm's length. "I could give you some-thing to take the edge off," he said. "There's no purple heart for bravery in these things."

Sylvia squeezed his hand. "Thanks," she said. "I'll be okay, but I'll call you."

Cory shook his head ruefully. "I doubt it," he said. "But good luck."

The idea was to put one foot in front of the other without regard to where she might be going, which was good because direction wasn't Sylvia's strong point right now. She couldn't sleep, couldn't eat, and whenever she thought of the children, who as yet only dimly understood the difference between the separation and one of Mitchell's many trips, she felt assaulted by guilt. She was sinking, flailing, and only one thing brought her onto firm ground: whenever she asked herself if she regretted leaving Mitchell, if she could possibly be mistaken in this, the answer was a resounding no. She knew she couldn't have stood one more night, one more lugubrious conversation about advancing age and the impossibility of change. Depression was an awful thing, but it was *his* depression, just as all the anxiety seemed to have settled for good between her shoulder blades. In a sense, the emotional burden of the divorce had been divided between them and she would simply have to live with her share.

She felt rather than heard the phone and reached for it, still asleep. It was Charlie Steinmetz. They had gone out once or twice since Mitchell left but she wasn't sure how serious she was about him. She wasn't sure she was ready to be serious about anyone. The timing could be all wrong on this. "I hope I'm disturbing you," Charlie Steinmetz said.

Sylvia tried to think. She *was* disturbed, there was no question about that, but it pre-dated the call. She wouldn't lay that at Charlie's feet. Then she realized what he had said. He *hoped* he was disturbing her? She laughed. "I don't think so," she replied. "Why would you want to disturb me?"

There was a hesitation. "Oh, Christ," Charlie said. "I was trying to do this right. I'm sorry. I meant I didn't want to disturb you with if you were with patients. Are you busy?"

Sylvia was lying on her office floor in the fetal position. She had no idea whether she had patients waiting outside or not. She couldn't remember how she had gotten here in the middle of the afternoon. Then it came back slowly. There had been a cancellation after lunch and she had lain on the rug to relax for a few minutes. Her back was aching again. She shook her head vigorously now to wake up. "No," she said, rising to a sitting position and running her free hand through her hair. "It's okay. I'm alone."

She realized dimly that she should have been more encouraging, that her voice should rise in pleasure at Charlie's call, that she should have a slight catch in her throat, something to indicate her delight at his unexpected call. She should seem pleased that he had thought of her. She could hear her mother's disapproving voice in her ear, and even see her standing just out of range pretending to be busy with some household chore while she criticized her phone manner, as she had on the few occasions when boys had called to ask Sylvia for dates in high school. 'Can't you pretend to be happy to hear from them?' her mother had asked. 'No, I can't,' Sylvia replied. 'And why should I anyway? They're creeps. I don't want them to call.'

But this wasn't high school. Amazing as it seemed sometimes, she was grown up, a physician, and she was responsible for two small children, more responsible than ever as far as that went. Whatever Mitchell's liabilities as a husband might have been, he always carried his weight concerning household chores and childcare. And she had loved this about him, his enthusiasm for the kids and childcare. She had been astonished when her lawyer told her he not only wasn't contesting custody, but wasn't asking for joint and might leave town. She had no idea how this would play with the kids when she finally told them, how Simon would put it together that his father, whom she had supposedly driven away, was now leaving all by himself. But she'd deal with that later on.

Okay, she told herself. Focus. Slow down. Evaluate the situation. Where the hell are we here? She looked at the phone as if it were a foreign object. Then, thankfully, it began to make sense. A man had called, an attractive man, someone she liked, someone she had even *hoped* would call. And he wasn't married, or not really married. What's more, he was a man whom she had seen before, which meant that she hadn't screwed it up the first time. This was all good. It should even be cause for celebration. She got up off the floor and cradled the phone between her shoulder and neck. Where were her shoes?

"I'm sorry," she said. "I'm just a little scattered today. It's really nice to hear from you."

Charlie didn't seem to notice any of this which made Sylvia wonder if he was nervous too. "I was just thinking," he said slowly, as if he was concentrating mightily on the words. "I mean, I was wondering if you'd like to have coffee? Or maybe dinner?"

It seemed like an important question, one put with appropriate gravity. Not the coffee or dinner or whatever it might eventually turn out to be, but the idea of starting out in life again. The fact that they had done this before would mean they were dating, she thought, but did one actually date at her age or was that too retro? If a friend asked, she could say she was *seeing* someone, and let the friend figure out what she meant by that. All at once, she felt more alive. "That would be great," Sylvia said, surprising herself with enthusiasm. "I'd really like that."

She appreciated Charlie's seriousness, even his awkward way of asking, even though they kind of knew each other, or at least weren't strangers. She wouldn't have wanted him to be practiced or smooth. She had been married for twelve years and in that time she had been mostly faithful, though she had wondered about Mitchell. There were those trips to England and everywhere else. She remembered his taking furtive glances at letters that would then disappear into a pocket or briefcase never to be seen again. Still, that was in the past and had nothing to do with this man, Charlie Steinmetz, who was waiting patiently for her to collect herself.

"Maybe this weekend," he said. "Friday or Saturday?"

"Either one," Sylvia said, "I'm real open." She wondered whether or not she should have said that, whether she should have acted as if she had a full social schedule. But she didn't care. She didn't want to play games with this man. "Whatever you want to do," she added. "It doesn't matter." Then it was done, or begun, with Charlie promising to come by on Friday. And Sylvia suddenly knew she had somehow achieved movement and her spirits began to lift.

Mr. Whitley was in the hospital. When Sylvia made rounds she found him with his leg supported in a sling and encased in a swath of blue cotton. The leg itself was engorged and an IV stand next to the bed was dispensing a continuous river of glucose. Yet the patient was in a good mood. One might even have described him as sprightly. "Guess there was something wrong after all, Doc," Whitley said, beaming. He winked at her, as if they were sharing some momentous secret.

Sylvia listened to the pulses in Mr. Whitley's leg and looked beneath the bandage. His knee was dwarfed by his white, swollen calf and the whole leg was an angry purple. "You seem to be pretty cheerful about it, Mr. Whitley," she said. "Are you in pain?"

"I knew there was something wrong," Whitley said gleefully, ignoring the question. "It's good to be right," he growled. "Doctors always think they know everything; no one ever listens to the goddamned patient."

Sylvia wondered idly if this would be the prelude to some kind of legal action. She thought again of the Moses and his pitiful wife in her faded housedress begging her to understand that her husband hadn't been serious when he sued her. She remembered Steffes and the M&M. But Whitley seemed smug and self-satisfied rather than angry. And though it was a peculiar reaction, Sylvia was content to let the man have his moment of triumph. "Well, Mr. Whitley, you *were* right this time," she said. "There's definitely a problem. Your leg shouldn't be swollen like this."

A woman, who Sylvia guessed was Mr. Whitley's wife, sat at the foot of the bed looking concerned. "Is it serious, Doctor?" she asked.

It was always serious to be hospitalized and phlebitis, if that's what this swelling turned out to be, was nothing to dismiss, but Sylvia wanted to reassure the woman and her patient. She knew that beneath the bluster and satisfaction of having proven her wrong, Mr. Whitley must be worried too. "I think we can get this under control," she said. "The important thing is that we've got Mr. Whitley on medication that will bring down the swelling. We've also given him anti-coagulants to guard against blood clots." She looked at the woman who now seemed visibly relieved. "I should have admitted him sooner."

It was good to admit guilt; cleansing for her and it almost always brought forth protestations from the patients to the effect that everyone made mistakes. At base they wanted their doctors to be right, wanted to believe in them, to feel secure in their knowledge and skill. It was one reason for the outrage at iatrogenic cases, when doctors made fatal errors. They weren't supposed to make mistakes, weren't supposed to be wrong. They were supposed to know the effects of every medication they prescribed as well as all the chemical interactions of those drugs with others the patients might be taking. They were supposed to keep up, read medical journals at night in between call and trips to the hospital. They were supposed to be infallible, in part because they had accepted it themselves in their arrogance and their presumption. Doctors were almost never humble in Sylvia's experience and this was often their downfall. Where medicine was concerned, failure was usually costly and to patients never merely an understandable mistake. It could never be a case of being overloaded, tired or inattentive, never a simple error in judgment; instead it was always a betrayal of essential faith. That was the deal; that was the emotional contract physicians had made with patients, nurses, hospitals, everyone.

And more than anything that was what had allowed the managed care system to develop as it had. Without the resentment and distrust the old system had created, insurance companies would be nowhere. Yet given what had happened, or might have happened, or had happened to someone else, now more than ever Sylvia believed it was important for patients to believe their doctor was committed to their well being, that someone cared.

Fortunately, Whitley was magnanimous in victory. "Don't worry about it, Doc," he said, laughing. "No one else caught it either. I was the only one." This actually made sense to Sylvia. Patients often knew more than their doctors suspected and the most sophisticated diagnostic tests were often wrong or inconclusive. Often the first hint of a serious condition was a patient's telling his doctor he just didn't feel right. Vague feelings of unease could be worth more than a dozen tests. Sylvia made a note on Mr. Whitley's chart and walked out of the ward.

Outside, she heard a voice."You're looking better." She turned to see Cory Weintraub.

"You sound disappointed," she said. But it was true. People often took strength from the misfortunes of others. She smiled to show she didn't think less of him for it.

"Not really," Cory said. "Like I said, what you're feeling is all pretty uncomplicated. Want to have lunch?"

They walked into the cafeteria and took a corner table. "What's going on?"

Despite herself, Sylvia blushed and looked away. "Not much," she said. "Nothing important. You?"

"Never lie to a shrink," Cory said. "You met someone, right?"

"Sort of," Sylvia said. "Actually, I already knew him." Then, quickly, like a school girl, "Not like that. I mean, I met him when I was working on a case. He's a professor, a writer."

She thought of Charlie Steinmetz' earnest expression, his large brown eyes, most of all his intensity. They were alike in that way.

Mitchell had always been baffled by this in her. "Why does everything have to be so intense with you?" he asked once, as if personality were a choice, something one selected at leisure. It wounded her at the time and for a period she tried to change, but now Sylvia thought that she liked intensity in others, the idea that things mattered, even little things. Perhaps eventually she would learn to like intensity in herself.

"Well, which is it," Cory said, a slight edge in his voice. "Professor or writer?" His reaction startled her. Something about this irritated him, Sylvia thought, perhaps that he had been right in saying that her depression was temporary, simple. Maybe all along he had hoped she would cycle down into something less benign and be committed to his care in some back ward at County. Which was bizarre, but then who could ever tell what anyone else really thought about anything.

"He teaches writing, but he also writes himself. Novels," Sylvia said. "I met him when another writer got sick while he was visiting at the University. Charlie signed him into the hospital and I ended up catching the case."

"Interesting," Cory said, his tone of voice suggesting that it was anything but that. Sylvia sympathized, but sometimes men were annoyingly transparent. They always needed to feel that there might be a chance for them with women even if it wasn't true. Cory wanted to believe that had it not been for the inconvenience of his having a wife Sylvia would have been willing to go off for a lost weekend in Aspen whenever he wanted, that it was *his* option. Which was ridiculous, but Sylvia knew it was harder to give up illusion than reality. Now Cory stood suddenly. "I've got a patient," he said abruptly, and was gone.

Sylvia sat at the table, alone but not lonely. She had more patients to see and the kids needed to be picked up but just for this moment she was going to ignore all that and enjoy doing nothing, attending to no one. There was a line at the cash register and when it loosened up she would rise and go and order an omelet and eat it slowly and then, eventually, she would leave and take up the life she had chosen for herself. But now, in this brief period before her life started again, she would focus on everything around her: the old couple at the next table deep in conversation about some awful decision; the children playing beneath their parents' table; the serious young interns with worried looks and lined foreheads; the nurses and orderlies moving with bored nonchalance through their routine of illness and death, knowing none of it would ultimately be their responsibility.

It was a world, not the best world no doubt, perhaps not even a very good one, but it was hers. She had made a place for herself here and she belonged. Now it seemed as if everyone she had ever treated, all the patients past and present had joined her at the table. Mr. Whitley sat across from her in earnest discussion with the Simmons family while Thomas Morris and the Moses talked about interpretations of the bible and sacred music. It was all a crazy mosaic of memory and while she watched the people real and imagined gathered round, she interacted with none of them. Whatever might happen to them, whether or not she could really help or lessen the pain, she knew she was the essential center, the nexus of this particular universe. She represented hope, where it made no sense to have any, comfort when it was needed, and her patients were destined to break her heart. But not here and not now.

In this moment before going to do rounds, she took stock. Sylvia Rose, physician and surgeon, Diplomate of the American Board of Neurology and Psychiatry and proprietor of a failed marriage, surveyed the world she had created and decided that she approved of what she had done. More, she embraced and celebrated it.

CHAPTER ELEVEN

B y the time Sylvia got to the hospital it was 4:15 and her patient
was in the ICU. The call came at 3:30 and at first she had not
understood what the nurse was saying. She had been dreaming
and in the fog of sleep Whitley had sounded like Whalley, who
had been her English teacher in high school. Tweed jackets and a
distracted air she had taken then for brilliance. She had loved him
until he patted her behind in the supplies closet one afternoon,
which broke the spell. Mr. Whalley. By now he was retired, if he was
even still alive.

"Could you repeat that?" Sylvia said to the nurse, banishing
thoughts of Dickens and the London fog from her mind. "I'm sorry. I didn't quite understand what you said."

The nurse coughed, signaling disapproval. Sylvia thought that
sometimes nurses enjoyed calling doctors in the middle of the
night, exercising this small power over those superior to them in
the medical hierarchy. Over the years, Sylvia had been awakened
for trivial reasons like approving the administration of Tylenol and

sleeping pills to patients, but this sounded serious. "I said Whitley," the nurse drawled. "He's your patient, right?"

Now Sylvia was wide awake. "Of course he's my patient. Is something wrong?"

"He threw an embolus," the nurse said. "We've sending him up to Intensive Care but I think you'd better come down and take a look."

Without asking how a patient who had been stable at ten o'clock could be in this situation six hours later, Sylvia threw on jeans and a sweatshirt and drove to the hospital. The night streets were shiny with water and the overhead lights made the shadows seem intriguing. She imagined that this was what others would consider dramatic about her job, speeding through the darkened city before dawn to save a life. Racing from the examining room to the OR while nurses yelled "Stat" at one another. Maybe. But for Sylvia the drama didn't exist. Rather, she thought of the children she had left behind in their beds, the hurried call to a disgruntled neighbor who had agreed to stay with them until her soon to be ex-husband could get over to the house. And beyond that the reality that she still had a full day in the office that she would now face on four hours of sleep. She tried to put all this out of her mind and concentrate on the patient. She wasn't very concerned about Mr. Whitley, but she seldom worried about patients in the personal way one would about a child or loved one. She had lost that during medical school and residency. It would do Mr. Whitley no good for her to feel anxious about his condition, but she was very curious about what had gone wrong because when she left the hospital he had been fine, sitting up in bed and making jokes about the nurses.

After parking in the physicians' lot, Sylvia took the elevator and entered her patient's room. She stood at the foot of the bed and scanned his chart quickly. The man was blue, unconscious, and his wife was wringing her hands just outside the tented area of the

ICU. According to the chart, he had been getting Heparin on an intravenous drip, which should have broken up any blood clots in his leg, but something had gotten free and lodged in his pulmonary artery which, Sylvia knew, meant it was a virtual certainty that Mr. Whitley would die, no matter what she or anyone else might do. She put down the chart and looked over at the nurse, a slight red-haired woman whom she hardly knew. Her nametag read Carolyn, so Sylvia said, "Bring me up to speed, Carolyn. What happened since I left last night?"

The nurse was very young and scared, as if she feared she was about to be blamed for something. It might be that she had never had a patient die before. "I looked in on him at dinner and he seemed okay, but then later on when we looked in he was real feverish, sweating and he was having trouble breathing."

"Why didn't someone call me then?"

It was an obvious question. Call when something might actually be done rather than waiting until the crisis. "The attending, Dr. Jenkins, he thought it was just that Mr. Whitley was tired. He'd been walking the ward and then he came back and put his feet up."

Whitley was a marathon runner. It seemed unlikely that walking around the hospital would have tired him out, but the attending wouldn't have known that. "He put his feet *up*? Sylvia said, incredulous. "And no one here stopped him?" You didn't want patients with phlebitis elevating their feet above their hearts, though in other cases of swelling it might have made some sense.

"No one saw him," the nurse wailed. "He was just in there watching the teevee with his wife, doctor."

Sylvia nodded, listening to her patient's stertorous breathing, which sounded oddly like a steam engine in the night. It was frustrating, but there wasn't much they could do now. When an embolus lodged in a major artery, the effect was similar to myocardial infarction: the supply of blood was cut off and in a short time tissue died and thus the patient. She had put Whitley on anti-coagulants to break up whatever clots might be in his leg, but there was always the chance that one would break off, and now this had happened. Surgery wasn't an option because there wasn't time and he was on Heparin which would make him bleed out if they opened him up. Sylvia walked to the head of the bed and took her patient's hand. It was lifeless, the fingers cold as sausage.

They remained that way for fifteen minutes until Whitley's body seized up suddenly, his mouth set in the rictus of death. Sylvia continued to hold his hand for a moment. Then she consulted her watch and turned to Carolyn. "Time of death is 5:06," she said, and laid Whitley's hand gently on the sheet. She lowered her head to the bed for a moment and closed her eyes. Poor Mr. Whitley, she thought. He'd been right, and so glad to be right, about what was wrong, but right or not, he hadn't been able to survive overnight in a first-class teaching hospital. She rose and looked at his lifeless body for a moment. Then she went outside to talk to his widow.

In the cafeteria at six AM, a plate of cold eggs in front of her, Sylvia remembered a time when the room would have been full, even at this hour with cooks in white aprons preparing the day's meals and baking muffins and bread. Now there were fewer patients, thanks to managed care, and fewer staff members in the hospital. There was only one cook, who sat waiting patiently for the few customers who would come through her line. Even this was better than most of the hospitals in town; Sylvia had often eaten an evening meal out of vending machines. They called what was happening to the cafeterias outsourcing; it was cheaper for the hospital to purchase services from independent companies than to employ their own kitchen staff. A small thing, these amenities, but it was the same as everything else in medicine and had the effect of making life more difficult; less human but cost-efficient. Did it matter if patients' families could get meals at any hour of the day or night while they waited to hear the fate of a loved one? Not to the bottom line, but Sylvia thought it probably made a difference to the families.

She thought of her late patient, how excited Mr. Whitley had been to have her discover that he was not a malingerer after all, how pleased that during her examination in the office Sylvia had missed the weakened vein that in the end led to his death. Even his wife was struck by her husband's gleeful celebration of his illness. When Sylvia had gone to talk to Mrs. Whitley outside the ICU, she said, "He was just so happy. I never knew anyone who needed so much to be right about things."

Which meant, of course, that Sylvia had been wrong, at least in the initial diagnosis. There would be an M&M during which a panel of doctors would review her process notes, but that didn't bother Sylvia. There ought to be an investigation when someone died, especially if there was the possibility of doctor's error, as there certainly had been in this case. She had done nothing that any other physician wouldn't have done and while she might have left a sign on his bed instructing one and all not to raise his feet, it was reasonable to assume that any attending would check the chart and see that the patient was suffering from phlebitis. It was a tragic error and someone had died who didn't need to, but there was nothing she could do about that. Sylvia reminded herself that Mr. Whitley had only come to her in the first place because other doctors had referred him. No one was right all the time. And once Whitley had been admitted, his treatment had been appropriate, if not heroic. Heroism hadn't been called for.

None of that was what bothered her. People got sick and died, even when they were in hospitals and received excellent care. The human body was built to fail eventually. That was undeniable. What nagged at Sylvia was the suspicion that the uproar in her personal life had clouded her judgment and made her less careful than she might otherwise have been.

Would she have been more thorough in her examination of Mr. Whitley, taken more time, if she hadn't been going through a divorce? Would she have been more patient with him and less willing to write off his anxieties as hypochondria if she hadn't known that she was late and it was her turn to drive the carpool? Would she have been more alert if she hadn't been sleep-deprived, if she hadn't been so anxious about the effects of the divorce on her children? And finally, would she have listened with greater attention to her patient if she hadn't been thinking about the new man with whom she was going to have dinner after she drove the carpool, assuming she could stay awake? It was impossible to say for sure and it wouldn't really matter if the patient hadn't died. But he had, and so it did, and this was what bothered her.

She looked down at the congealed mess on her plate. She remembered sitting in this same room twelve hours earlier and having the fleeting feeling of control and mastery. It was gone now, replaced by a gnawing pain in the pit of her stomach. She was aware of someone beside her and when she looked up Cory Weintraub was standing there. Did this man ever go home?

"We don't usually see you so early," Cory said. "May I?" He indicated the empty chair next to her.

"Go ahead," Sylvia said. "What are you doing here at this hour anyway?"

"People have a way of committing suicide at odd hours," he said. "But why do I always get the impression you'd rather I was someone else."

"I'm sorry, Cory," Sylvia said. She pressed his hand on the table. "It's been kind of a hard night."

Cory nodded. "I heard you lost one," he said.

His casual language irritated Sylvia. It was the way doctors talked, especially male doctors, taking pride in their lack of feeling, eschewing any sentiment over the loss of life. The patient had checked out, they would say, or they had punched his ticket. When a patient with multiple, life-threatening problems was admitted to the hospital, he was called a train wreck. And someone without adequate insurance was a Gomer, which was an acronym for Get Out of My Emergency Room.

It was all a kind of systematic desensitization to human suffering, which was probably intended to protect the doctors from caring too much but ended up as a kind of natural selection for callousness among physicians. Even the battlefield expressions people commonly used annoyed Sylvia, saying that the patient had fought hard but lost his battle against, take your pick, cancer, heart disease, ALS, anything. None of it made sense to her. Illness wasn't strategic, though timing was vital. But if disease had progressed beyond a certain point it didn't matter how hard you fought, prayed, laughed, or loved. If everything went wrong, you died, and in the end everything would go wrong for everyone. Attitudes were overrated, she thought, but none of that was Cory's fault. "He threw a clot," Sylvia said now. "Nothing we could do."

Cory was immaculately dressed, as always, the expensive clothes almost successful in disguising the fact that he was a short, pudgy man who was losing his hair. "You want to talk about it?" he asked.

She didn't, but Sylvia knew Cory was trying to be sympathetic and didn't deserve her short responses. "I was just wondering whether or not I'd be a better doctor if I wasn't a single mother with an estranged husband who's an asshole and a new boyfriend I don't know much about yet."

"Mitch's got a boyfriend?" Cory asked with new interest.

This made Sylvia smile. "I meant me," she said. "But who knows?" Now she began to feel a little more hopeful. "Your patients die, don't they?"

"Not as often as I'd like," Cory said. Then, "Sorry, I don't mean to make light of it, but in a practice like mine they come and go all the time. They terminate, then come back, suicide sometimes, more often they just make lame tries at it."

"Terminate?" Sylvia said.

"In psychiatry it just means they've stopped their treatment; it can be a good thing if something actually changes and they're doing better. But most of the time patients are back in six months with some new problem, or a new wrinkle on the same old thing."

"I guess Mr. Whitley terminated his treatment too," Sylvia said, "but it wasn't his choice." She ate a mouthful of eggs. "I've got to go," she said. "Thanks, Cory. This helped."

"What did I do?"

"Nothing, everything. I don't know. See you later."

The children were off to school by the time Sylvia got home and Mitchell had gone too. She figured she just had time to shower and change clothes before she had to turn around and go back to the hospital for morning rounds. Still she was glad she had made the effort to come home instead of just staying downtown. This way she could at least pretend it was a normal day in a normal life.

Mitchell had left a note on a monogrammed card that was leaning against a coffee cup at her place at the table. It was silly but she still hoped for certain things from him, gestures that might indicate that at least it had made sense to be married to him at one time. But the note lacked intimacy or even warmth. "Syl," it read. "I'm glad I was able to help you out, but in the future I'd appreciate it if you'd try to plan a little better. I do have a life of my own."

Sylvia examined the card closely now. It was thick and off-white on some kind of linen stock. She knew that Mitchell wouldn't have used it unless he was trying to make a point, tell her something. When they were living together, they had corresponded on the backs of envelopes or torn edges of placemats. Since when had linen cards come into the equation, assuming there even was an equation anymore? She wondered not for the first time how she could ever have been married to this man. And what did he mean by planning better? Who planned an emergency, a terminal illness? She turned the card over and read it again. He made it sound as if his coming over the night before had been an enormous imposition. Of course she knew it was inconvenient, but these were his children too, even if she had been granted custody by the court. She wasn't asking a favor of a friend.

She tossed the card in the garbage can where it lay among the coffee grinds and orange peels. She knew that part of her irritation was a remnant of the marriage. Even though it was over, she hadn't stopped wanting Mitchell to act like a man whom she might respect, a person her children could admire and look to for help. She knew she had to give that up, and for the most part she had, but it was a process. She no longer badgered Simon to call his father on special occasions, and had stopped worrying that Becky was too solicitous of Mitchell's hurt feelings. She had stopped prompting Mitchell to call when one of the kids had done well in school or was involved in an activity. And she had nearly put aside her fear that in the end his occasional extravagances would cause them to love him more than they did her. Despite these adjustments, however, her feelings were slow to change, and now she wondered if they ever would, or if that peculiar reaction to the man would always remain with her regardless of what became of them in their lives apart. She sighed in the quiet room. It was time to terminate with Mitchell, long past time, but it was proving more difficult than Sylvia might have wanted.

She put some dishes in the sink and ran water over them. The kitchen, like the rest of the house, was a haphazard record of their lives together. The mismatched oven mitts, the dishes, pots and pans, even the orange tile on the floor that she had never liked. To her, it all spoke of her inability to make conscious decisions as a couple. Things had happened; he would have said they evolved. But Sylvia didn't think anything had ever reached a higher level; time, their lives together, had just gone by. And now it was all over and she was left with a sink full of dirty dishes when she was late to work. She went upstairs to dress.

The appearance of routine in medicine was in part artificial because while the doctors and nurses moved through their daily rounds calmly, scheduling X-rays, procedures and surgery, none of this would ever be ordinary to their patients. It was the essential dislocation between those who were sick and those with the responsibility to care for them. Sylvia knew this and tried to keep it uppermost in her mind as she saw patients, but today it was difficult. A man had died, she hadn't slept, and Mitchell's note continued to work away at her despite her determination to put it behind her and stay in the present.

At noon she received some good news when she learned that she need not be present at the M&M for Mr. Whitley. Since the house staff had been responsible for his direct care when he went into crisis, the attending physician would be the one interviewed by the panel. If they needed more information, they would be in touch with her later, but Sylvia doubted she would hear anything more about the matter officially. There would be an autopsy, but she doubted anything new would be revealed. The cause of death was obvious. There was also a call from Charlie Steinmetz on her voice mail.

Sylvia delayed returning Charlie's call, though she wasn't sure why. She liked him more each time she saw him and their relationship had grown to the point that they had slept together, something that had seemed daunting to her when she thought about it because of her long marriage to Mitchell. She had worried that Charlie would disapprove of her functional underwear or the fact that she hadn't had her legs waxed lately. She had imagined he would think her unfeminine, yet the idea of going out and buying frilly underthings or taking a spa day in preparation for a date seemed like an overreaction. Sex was a part of herself that she had once valued but which had atrophied in the years with Mitchell to the point that it seemed more like a chore than something to be anticipated and fussed over.

She wondered if there were innovations of which she would be ignorant, new sexual moves she should know. Certainly the dating scene had changed in the fifteen years she had been married, though she had never been part of any scene when she was single. She wondered if she should buy a book on the subject and get up to speed, or perhaps review the *Kama Sutra*. Someone had told her the whole thing, along with illustrations, was now online. It would do no harm to be informed since in this, as in all things, she wanted to excel. Yet that seemed inimical to the whole idea of sex, which was, after all, supposed to be free and spontaneous. In the end, Sylvia had found making love to Charlie to be both relaxing and reassuring. It was easy, like descending into a warm bath. Still, she found that she was reluctant to bring him home with her or even invite him for dinner and she wasn't sure why since the kids were curious.

It occurred to her that she might be protecting Mitchell from the inevitable comparisons the children would make, but in the moment of thinking this she realized that whatever his inadequacies as a man might be, biology gave Mitchell a nearly insurmountable advantage over Charlie or anyone else she might meet and fall in love with. The incumbent would always be the favorite in parental matters and the kids would more likely hate Charlie for breaking up their happy home than run to him with open arms. So her hesitation didn't have to do with that, but then what was it all about?

She had never really been interested in feminism, not even during her college days when everyone paid homage to those ideas, but Sylvia knew she had lived out a sort of feminist ideal, intentional or not in her personal and professional lives. She had defied her father and a hostile medical school dean who felt women merely took places away from deserving men with families to support. She had gone through two pregnancies without interrupting her internship or residency. Whatever her nighttime doubts about her own worth, she knew there were young women medical students who regarded her as some kind of role model. All of this came at a price, of course, and to be fair, Mitchell had paid part of it. A more assertive husband might have demanded more of her, more time, more attention. Now that he was gone, things would be simpler, except of course, for Charlie.

But just as it would be unfair to blame Mitchell entirely for the divorce, Sylvia knew that as nice, attractive, sexy and interesting as Charlie Steinmetz was, he was also ballast. Whatever Mitchell's faults may have been, Sylvia hadn't had to think about that part of her life while they were married, and now she did. She knew the answer was not simply to find another man to plug into Mitchell's empty space and go on. It annoyed her that she'd even think of Charlie that way, yet structurally that's where he would fit in her life. Even if she did care for him and it turned out they had some kind of future together, he was serving a function now: to reassure Sylvia that despite being on the cusp of middle-age and burdened with children, she was still desirable, attractive and interesting to a man who presumably had other options.

What she knew was that it was pleasant to have a new life and to have a man be part of it without wondering if he was what she'd been waiting for all this time. It seemed predictable to think the first requirement of a recently divorced woman should be to find a man as quickly as possible, but that didn't mean she had to be celibate. Even if the psychologist in Boulder was right about starter husbands, there was no guarantee that her next step in matrimony would be any more successful than the first had been.

For as long as she could remember Sylvia had felt the pressure to move somewhere, be with someone, to do something and do it fast. What she wanted most now was just to slow down and look around. She thought again of the yoga teacher: Breathe and relax; relax and breathe. The asana she liked best intuitively was Utkatasana, also called awkward pose, but the word meant intense in Sanscrit. Now Sylvia decided to learn to like something else.

She knew that she would call Charlie and in the end, after their lives settled down into some kind of routine, they might end up together. Still, it was pleasant to think that there was nothing urgent about this. She didn't *have* to do anything immediately. There were no decisions hanging imminently over her head. She didn't have to be intense about this; in fact, it might work out better if she wasn't.

Back in her office, Sylvia put on her white coat and looked at the day's schedule that lay nicely printed on her desk. Patients with their lives in various stages of disarray were scheduled through five o'clock, but despite her early morning call, Sylvia's head was clear and it did not seem quite as overwhelming as it had before. She had only three people in the hospital and there were no emergencies. As an added bonus, the kids were scheduled to be with Mitchell for the evening, linen cards or not. She was free to concentrate on patients who needed her help without worrying about the car pool and then go her own way. She could call Charlie or perhaps a girlfriend and go to a movie. Or she could stay home and eat Chinese food out of a cardboard container and call no one. She didn't know and it didn't concern her that she didn't know. This seemed like a revolutionary development.

Sylvia felt a vague anxiety about the future, about what would become of her and her children. The idea that she was their primary source of support, even if Mitchell had given her little in the past seemed like an awesome responsibility. And she wasn't sure about her future in medicine. She liked what she did and knew she was good at it, but losing a patient was bound to make you doubt yourself. How would she feel if more and more of her decisions were questioned by gatekeepers who cared about the bottom line rather than the terrified people who crowded her office every day? What if the structure of medical practice were to dictate that patients be seen primarily by physicians' assistants or nurses who had less training than doctors, but cost less? It was already happening in some specialties and Sylvia imagined that the problems Thomas Morris had encountered were likely to become routine and doctors would be forced to become advocates to a greater extent than they already were.

She could fight the good fight, as she had; she could protest to case managers and effect small changes for a few patients in certain situations. But in the end, so what? In a fundamental sense, what would have changed? More to the point, what would be the effect on her of trying hard and failing over and over again? Some doctors, like Luther, were just giving up their practices, quitting as a matter of principle, but that didn't have much impact as a protest and it changed nothing. Besides, she was too young to do that, and she had the kids.

In the moment of thinking this, however, Sylvia found she was feeling more determined than discouraged. She knew she would keep on doing what she was doing not only because it was what she had trained to do, but because even in this environment, it was important work. She helped people and sometimes changed lives by doing things in a certain way. And if her ability to help was limited by the nature of illness or if in some cases, like Mr. Whitley's she didn't help at all, it didn't matter to her in the end. Whoever said life shouldn't be frustrating or contradictory? She would just have to learn to manage with managed care and not let it or the tragic situations of her patients defeat her. She thought she could do that. And that would have to be enough.

CHAPTER TWELVE

Endings seldom seemed to finally end anything, at least for Sylvia. Patients came in and out of her life and while she did her best to help, no, to save them all, the reality was that more often she had to settle for ameliorating their suffering. There were few cures for those with neurological illnesses and fewer happy endings. Patients moved on and so she had to as well, but some stayed with her, like Mr. Whitley and Thomas Morris, though for different reasons.

She had made mistakes both in diagnosis and in treating Mr. Whitley and while they might not have led directly to his death, Sylvia continued to go over the case in her mind. Thomas was different. On the face of it, his condition was much worse than Whitley's and yet she had not been willing to accept this in caring for him, choosing to explore experimental protocols wherever she could find them. She had fought the case worker to get medication for Thomas that wasn't on the formulary of his insurance company and still he had gotten progressively worse to the point that he was now on bed rest, which they were pretending wouldn't be his permanent disposition.

She had dropped by his house this morning and now they were sitting in a sunny parlor where the furniture had been pushed aside to make room for a hospital bed. Thomas was propped up on pillows and his right hand was splinted to allow him enough control to turn pages in a book, drink coffee or switch television channels. The progress of the disease had been fast and brutal. There was no other word.

Thomas' wife had come in briefly and then left them alone. Sylvia couldn't be sure but she sensed a distance between her and Betsy and thought there might be some resentment there. She didn't blame the woman. Even if there was no fault and no reason, it was human nature to want to hold someone responsible in a tragic situation and ironically the patients for whom she'd done the most were often the least grateful. Sylvia didn't mind. Against reason, she agreed with Betsy and blamed herself for Thomas' decline. Still, he had called and asked to see her and she couldn't refuse.

"Your color is good," she said, not knowing what else to say.

"Small victories," Thomas said. "I was always good at make-up."

"You used make-up for concerts?"

"Not all of them. Only the ones that were televised." Thomas smiled weakly at his joke.

"How are you feeling?" Sylvia asked. Even if most medical options had been exhausted she couldn't help being a doctor.

Thomas shrugged. Few patients had his *sang froid,* fewer still were able to maintain a sense of humor when seriously ill. "I've discovered the internet," he said. "I was never interested in it before but there's an amazing variety of services available on line these days."

Sylvia's expression gave her away and Thomas laughed. "Not those kinds of services," he said. He gestured toward the lower half of his body. "They wouldn't do me much good anyway."

Sylvia smiled. "So what have you been investigating?"

"I'm taking contract bridge lessons from a shut-in in Kentucky," Thomas said. "And I've been watching horse races in California. It's wonderful to see the strength and speed of those animals."

"But not betting on the races, I hope."

He shook his head. "So far I'm just admiring what I can't do," Thomas said. "I'm not interested in handicapping. To me, they're all winners."

Sylvia looked around the parlor, which had taken on the look of a sick room with regimental lines of pill bottles and gifts that had yet to be opened. A wheelchair was against the wall and the rugs had been pulled back to allow Thomas room to maneuver when he got up from his bed. Now she went to the bed and performed a perfunctory exam on her patient. She checked the pulses in his arms and legs and looked to make sure his throat was clear. Patients as sick as Thomas often suffocated when the muscles in their throats relaxed completely.

When she stepped back, Thomas said, "So I'll make it for a while longer?"

"Doctors hate to be pinned down," Sylvia said and smiled.

"I know," Thomas said. "Insurance, right? Malpractice and all?"

"I'm not worried," Sylvia said. Then she patted his shoulder and sat down again. It was hard to believe this was the same man she'd heard in concert at the University a little over a year ago.

As if he had read her mind, Thomas said, "I was just thinking of the day you came here and played for Betsy and me."

Sylvia blushed involuntarily. She remembered the invitation and being surprised by the big house in Country Club, the wide portico and spacious wood floors covered with oriental rugs. She'd never played a really good piano before and had been more than a little intimidated by Thomas sitting and listening to her. She'd played Schuman, "Kinderszenen," she remembered. One of the few pieces she knew by heart. "I don't think I was very good," she said.

Thomas waved her objections aside. "You were fine, but the main thing is I could see you were serious about it, very serious. I liked that."

"That's always been my problem," Sylvia said. "Too serious." She thought of Mitchell asking why everything had to be so intense with her.

"That's ridiculous," Thomas said. "That's like being too rich. Anyway, the reason I wanted to see you today was that I have a present for you. I'd like to give you my piano. You've been a wonderful doctor but more than that, you've been a great friend and I appreciate it."

Sylvia thought of the gleaming Chickering in the next room and felt tears form in her eyes. "Oh, you can't do that," she said. "It's incredibly generous, but you don't have to do that."

Thomas nodded. "I know, but I want to. Betsey doesn't play and we don't have children. I could give it to the school, but I'd rather you had it. I think you said you're never had a decent piano. Isn't that right?"

It was true and it was one of the grudges she'd long held against her parents. Maybe she could give that up now. "Are you sure?"

"I won't be playing anymore. Whatever happens with the disease, I think we both know that."

Sylvia rose again and went to his bedside. She leaned over and kissed her patient. Then she caressed his cheek, where the redness from the Malar Rash was still visible. Tears came to her eyes and she thought she really was in love with this man. It was a different kind of love, but still love. "I don't know what to say."

"In situations like this, it's best not to say anything," Thomas said. "You'll never say too much or say the wrong thing. We do need to know your home address for the piano movers. They want to bring it by next week."

Despite her anxieties, the divorce went through more easily than Sylvia would have imagined. Tony's questionnaire never came up again so whether or not she and Mitchell were co-dependent would have to remain one of life's small mysteries. Sylvia bought Mitchell out of the house at an inflated price to salve her conscience and she got the better of the two cars, a ten year old Volvo. Starting over at her age might not be ideal but she knew it was better than waiting another twenty years to reach an inevitable conclusion. She hadn't heard from Gregory since the papers were signed but she hoped their periodic lunches would continue.

After waiting six weeks, Sylvia invited Charlie Steinmetz over for dinner to meet the kids. She didn't tell them anything other than that Charlie was a new friend of hers, but they weren't fooled. Simon knew a possible replacement, if not for his father then for his place of primacy in the house. When Charlie came in, the boy stood back from the door and looked Charlie over carefully. Then he said, "If we called the police, would they come over and take you away?"

Sylvia was about to say something but Charlie held up his hand. "It's okay," he said. "It's a fair question." Then he turned to Simon. "I don't really know," he said. "Maybe. You want to call and see? Here, I'll do it for you." He picked up the handset and made a show of dialing 911.

It wasn't what Simon had expected but turned out to be exactly the right thing to do as the boy started laughing uproariously. "No, no," he said. "It's okay. Don't call them."

Charlie held the handset up. "You sure?" he said. "I'd actually kind of like to know myself." Then he smiled and replaced it in the cradle. Crisis averted. Sylvia wasn't sure if she loved Charlie but watching him with Simon she knew she could love him, and that was enough for now.

In the end, Sylvia is back in her office, high above the street, waiting in the quiet before her day of seeing patients will begin. She walks to the window and looks down. Somehow spring has come without her noticing. Buds are on the trees and in the beds in front of the office brilliant daffodils and tulips hesitantly push their way into the air. People are walking around in pastel colors and shorts and Sylvia thinks she probably needs a new wardrobe. She likes thinking that there is a natural rhythm in the world that's unaffected by the chaos in her personal life. She's aware of a new calmness and wonders if perhaps the biofeedback actually made a difference despite the mad scientist and his lab or perhaps because of him.

She walks around the room, picking up small objects and re-placing them, examining a picture of Gregory as a young man in a white coat, stethoscope around his neck. She touches the edges of the surfaces with her fingertips and then resettles herself in her chair. Soon her phone will start ringing and patients will fill her waiting room but for now there's the morning stillness to comfort her.

In the distance she can see the articulated wall at the horizon, as complex and puzzling as ever, pointing the way up to some un-known ideal, but for the first time instead of simply noticing it and turning away, Sylvia decides to walk down Broadway during her lunch hour and take a closer look at the sculpture. There might be more there to see than she has previously imagined.

Printed in Great Britain
by Amazon

25934372R00116